Rent (minus) Control

Turning Thirty

R.B. Winters

ISBN-13: 978-0615957272
ISNB-10: 0615957277

First Printing: June 2014

DEDICATION

People will always come and go, but if you're very lucky, a handful will always be there through the good, the bad and the funny. This book is for them.

Table of Contents

Rent (minus) Control

1. Queens

A heavy hand hit my back with a thump, Eric, or Business as I called him, plopped down on the stoop beside me.

"What are you doing out here alone?" Business asked, clearly beginning to feel the full effect of the vodka by his ear-to-ear grin.

"Just taking a quick breather. With that many people packed into your apartment it feels like we're in Chinatown."

Business laughed, shaking his head at my intolerance.

"Don't stay out here too long, it's almost time to cut the cake."

"Have you decided on a birthday wish?"

"Can I wish to be twenty-nine for another year?" Business scoffed, picking at the cracked black paint adorning the stoop's railing currently supporting his head.

"If that's your wish, maybe go younger, say twenty-five?"

"In that case, why not be twenty-one again?" Business proposed.

"Because we were poor and crazy."

"Right, now we're semi-poor and crazy, is that better?"

"Good point. Twenty-one it is." I knew when to admit defeat.

While we conversed I felt for some reason that I should be holding a cigarette. I don't smoke, nor do I want to, but it seemed as Business crossed the threshold of thirty and I was approaching the line, smoking somehow fit...or at least the slender stick would fit well as an accessory to my fingers.

"Can you believe we're thirty?"

"You're thirty, don't drag me down too."

Turning thirty never bothered me; in fact the idea of getting away from my twenties is appealing in many ways. That was until a few months ago. Business began counting down to his birthday, as well as mine. Though he's slightly older, I think it gave him some comfort to instill fear in me. Business was terrified of turning thirty, as if it suddenly meant we were different people.

"Just four months and you'll be right here with me."

An eye roll and a head-bob was all I could muster. The truth, the more Business reminded me that I was about to be thirty, the more I panicked. It felt as though so many life goals that had yet to be met and I was behind my peers. I found myself applying and getting into grad school at the end of last year, in for the spring semester; not that I needed the degree, but in my head a Masters would mean something...right?

"Anyway, come back in soon or Brandon will eat all of the cake."

"You're the nicest brother," I remarked, giving a loaded side stare.

"It's not my fault I was the one that got the good genes, the least he could do is climb on a treadmill once in a while."

"He lives on Long Island, does it really matter if you have a gut out there, who's looking?"

"Yeah, but still, who wants to have a gut?"

Business left me with these words of wisdom, propping open the building door so I'd be able to enter without buzzing.

Up two flights and through the door I could hear a festive crowd laughing as music played something upbeat in the background. Pushing open the door with excess care, attempting to avoid knocking anyone or their drink over, I shoved my way back into the mob. The cake was just being placed on the table, Business sitting before the massive sheet of white frosting.

The limited space meant we were packed around the cake, had we been naked this would be the perfect opening scene to an orgy. Business' brother hovered over him, it may have been my imagination, but I could swear he was licking his lips like a ravenous wolf bottom at the sight of the cake.

A drunken rendition of happy birthday rang through the crowd, some of the gays hitting extra high notes to one-up each other; that or they were Off-Broadway performers. As the song concluded, I pounded a beer to drown out the voices, the phone in my pocket vibrating: *New Text Message from Dimitri.*

When the Animator moved to California he left a friend vacuum of sorts. Several people I had met and enjoyed going out with were only connected to me through the Animator. Upon his departure I made it my mission to collect the friends he left behind and build relationships outside of the bar.

Dimitri was one of the first I made an attempt to befriend. This worked out well as it caused a domino effect and cemented my friendship with several other people left in the Animator's wake. Including Larry, another Astoria local. The text message was an invitation to Larry's birthday, conveniently just down the street. It seemed everyone was getting older tonight.

Business was clearly preoccupied by other friends; a group around him, shoving well wrapped presents in his face. Being the good friend that I am, rather than provide useless junk that would be returned, my gift was chilling in the freezer for consumption whenever the party ran low on vodka or Business had some personal time. Slipping out the door and avoiding a public goodbye, I did a quick Google search to find my way, Queens isn't exactly familiar territory.

What would have been an easy train ride, was actually a considerable walk, my phone lied as usual, but I made it to the party. Larry's apartment was at least three times the size of mine. I had no idea apartments like this still existed off of Park Avenue at prices normal people could afford. The crowd was eclectic, loud and drunk. All the signs of a well-rounded party.

"You made it!"

Dimitri greeted me, taken by surprise as I was still examining the surroundings. A quick hug and Dimitri shuffled me around the room; introducing me to several people I was likely never going to see again, except for one, his mother. Instantly, I liked this woman, there was so much of my mom there.

As she danced with a gay a quarter her age, she held a drink in one hand and a cigarette in the other. The guy was going low, showing his flexibility and providing the crowd a cheap thrill as they whistled and cheered. Someone would surely take him home tonight.

"Mom, this is my friend, Ryan."
"Who?"
"Ryan, nice to meet you," I said, extending a hand.

Much to my amusement she came in for a hug, invading my space and still moving to the rhythm. If I closed my eyes this could absolutely be my mother, the life of the party.

"I need a drink, where's the kitchen?" I asked, breaking free of the mommy hold.

"Past the door, just down the hallway," Dimitri instructed, his mom returning to her original dance partner.

Pushing my way into the slender kitchen, bottles of booze lined the counter to the left, cups and cakes on the right. Two girls stood in the center of the room, blocking my way, deep in conversation. The type of conversation with importance defined by the amount of alcohol a person consumes. Something about cheating boyfriends and men being idiots. If I was as many drinks in, it's likely I'd join in their conversation to reaffirm that everything they think is tragically true.

Maneuvering past them to thumb through bottles and find something that wouldn't lay me out, I cringed as a bottle of Apple Pucker came into sight. When I was eighteen and under the influence of a deadly apple martini, I had fallen up a set of stairs, busting my nose and giving it a noticeable bump at the bridge. The goal is to one-day remove the bump through the hands of a talented surgeon and with it the memory of broken bones and bleeding on a bathroom floor. But until there's an extra ten ground in my bank account, I'll stick to avoiding apple anything.

Shaking the memory and taste from my mind, Grey Goose made its way into a cup and to my lips. One of the few types of vodka that were enjoyable, lacking the familiar hairspray taste of cheaper brands. Focus quickly shifted as an argument came from the hallway, followed by the slamming of a door.

"What's going on?" I asked as Dimitri slumped in the kitchen doorway.

"Josh just took off."

Dimitri began dating a ginger guy a few weeks back. Definitely cute, but gingers gave me the creeps and reminded me that I was a half ginger. A fact I could conceal as long as my facial hair was trimmed daily.

"Your friend, Shew, told him we're dating."
"You're dating, Shew?" I asked, puzzled. Who invited him?
"No, he just told Josh that to be an asshole and cause drama."

That definitely sounded like Shew, he had a magical way of causing drama and then acting as though he'd done nothing wrong. It was one of the reasons we only got together on occasion, a sociopath is a dangerous friend; you never know if they're about to screw you over or cause a scene. Larry appeared from the living room, grasping Shew's arm.

"You need to leave."
"What did I do?" Shew asked, looking truly perplexed.
"I have no idea, but Mark won't speak to me," Larry was fuming; I'd never seen him angry.

I'd been in the apartment no more than ten minutes and in that span of time Shew, who apparently wrangled an invite, managed to piss off four people, impressive.

"Dimitri," Larry looking to Dimitri, asking him through tone to eject the disruption.

"I'll walk him out," I interjected, sitting my drink on the white and blue speckle countertop.

"You don't need to go, he can walk himself out," Dimitri spat, giving Shew the evil-eye.

"It's ok, I'm not really in the party mood." It was true going home sounded like the best idea even though I'd just arrived.

Opening the door, Shew and I exited. This was typical behavior and I could almost hear exactly what he was going to say as we exited the building.

"What was all that about?" Shew asked.

There it was, that classic inability to accept responsibility or admit the mess made was calculated and not in any way accidental.

"Why do you do that shit?"

"Do what? I was just talking to them."

"Four people are pissed and you're the root, I think that's more than just friendly conversation."

"I don't know why they're mad."

"Whatever, it doesn't matter. Are you heading back to the city?" I asked, ready to drop the issue.

"I'm going to meet a friend at Albatross, wanna go?"

"I'll pass." Albatross was a dive bar I wasn't drunk enough to enter.

Parting ways, Shew headed up the street, likely to cause more mischief, as I made my way to the train. Climbing the stairs to the N train platform I waited in the warm early summer air. It wasn't long before the rickety silver train cars arrived and whisked me back to the city. One transfer, a short walk and I could see my building ahead, all that stood between was this one intersection.

Waiting for the streetlight to change a cab idled beside me, the window rolling down and from the corner of my eye I could see a hand gesture. Turning, a guy motioned for me to take out my earbud.

"Can I help you?" I asked, assuming he was a tourist about to ask where something was. *Ask the damn driver.*

"Would you like to grab dinner sometime?" the stranger asked.

"What?" This was not the question I'd expected.

The light changed and from the cab window the dark haired stranger extended a hand offering his business card. I accepted the card, watching, befuddled, as the cab disappeared into the night.

2. WelCome

My morning ritual was simple: Wake up, get dressed, make my hair look less like a heap, brush teeth and go to Starbucks. Starbucks was the motivating factor that encouraged me to enter the world each morning, rather than remain in the pile of blanks that was all too comfortable.

It was my short walk home, with latte in hand, which made today different. Standing at the front of my building examining the list of door buzzer names was the Animator.

"You'll never find me on there."

The Animator looking up, his face contorted with frustration.

"Thank god, I can't for the life of me remember your apartment number."

"It's 4D, like the man boobs I wish I had, and as far as the landlord is concerned my last name is Gutierrez. Also, I've always wondered why do Atheists say, *'thank god?'* Shouldn't there be a special expression for the non-believers among us?"

"How have they not updated the list? It's not as though you moved in yesterday. And we Atheists buy into mainstream expressions in order to appease the masses."

"This building has a lot of turnover. I've been here two years, making me a long-term resident. I'm sure they expect me to leave at any moment. Wise choice on the expression conformism."

"So your building is like a fancy whorehouse."

"It also smells better than most," I smirked.

Upstairs, the Animator sat his roller bag in the corner, plopping on the sofa. A sofa I was particularly proud of: The soft brown cloth and low arms were perfect for planting your face and ass after a long day or a hard night of drinking. It also doubled as the perfect place to unload problems.

"Don't take offense to this, I'm always happy to see you, but why are you here? I mean, you haven't been back in almost a year."

"I can't take living in California," confessed the Animator.

"I thought you were loving the job?" This was an unexpected twist.

"No, I've been faking it."

"Care for a drink and elaboration?"

"Yes, something strong please."

"Since I don't have a coffee pot, and I'm not sharing mine, I'm hoping you'll settle for vodka."

"Lots please."

Pouring the Animator a healthy portion of *life's cure for everything* and topping off my coffee with a shot, I took a seat next to him, positioning myself to receive a heavy load of gossip.

"When I moved to California, I told myself to try and make it work for two years and then see how I feel," explained the Animator.

"It's not been two full years."

"I know, but I can't take it any longer. I mean work is fine, it's the people."

"You mean their sun-kissed happiness?"

"Smart-ass. But in all seriousness, they are unfortunately happy and it's as fake as their bleach blonde hair and silicone boobs."

"Not to state the obvious, but, *duh*. What did you think it would be like out there? Stereotypes come from reality."

"The reality is that I'm done and back."

"Welcome home, should we plan a parade in your honor?"

"Just a small one, nothing flashy."

It was nice to know the Animator was back and not just visiting for a long weekend. I missed his snarky commentary.

"Where do you plan to live, didn't you sublet your apartment?"

"That's why I'm here. Can I stay on your couch for a while? At least until I find a place to live or evict my tenant."

"Of course."

"Thanks, I appreciate it."

"What are friends and sofas for if you can't sleep on them?"

"Cute. But tell me what's going on with you, I don't want to talk about my misery."

This was a loaded question. My life has become incredibly dull. I wrote my blog, worked on a new book and slept. That was about it these days.

"Not a lot, just writing and going through the motions."

"Seriously, you're not dating anyone, or at least sleeping around?"

"Not at the moment," I confessed.

"You became boring."

"But now I have you back to help mix things up."

"As long as it doesn't end up in a book." The Animator didn't mind my writing, though he wasn't a big fan of being within the pages.

"Should I lie to you?" I asked, all time spent together was fair game for sharing.

"Yes, please."

"I wouldn't dream of writing about you...unless I see the opportunity for personal gain."

"God I love you, I'm so glad to be back around cynical people with self-interest."

"That's New York."

The Animator unpacked the parts of his life that with within a bag, shoving clothing into my already bursting closet.

"Who's Leo?" he called.

"Who?" I asked, poking my head out from the bathroom.

"Leo. There's a business card here by the TV."

"Oh, it's some guy that gave me his card last night."

"Is he hot? Are you going to fuck him?" the Animator was clearly starved for the fast pace hookups the city offered.

"Calm down, I have no idea. I can barely remember his face. He gave me the card and asked me to dinner as his cab went by last night."

"That's sexy, like an urban fairy tale or some shit."

"You know, you swear a lot more than you used to," I pointed out.

"I know, it's all that time in fucking idiotville. I had to do something that would get a rise out of those hippie tree fuckers."

The Animator's mouth was definitely giving me a run for my money. Not that I didn't swear, but I liked to place words in a person's ear when I knew it would get a reaction, or I was dumbstruck, whichever came first.

"Are you going to go out with him?"

"I don't know, hadn't really thought about it."

"I say go. Have an adventure, it'll give you something to write about that doesn't include me."

He made a good point. Along with my dry spell, came boring blogs about things like people on the street and why I hate baristas that speak to one another instead of serving customers in an efficient manner.

"Maybe I will," I said, taking the card from the Animator's hand.

"I'm going to head out for a bit, will you be around later?" The Animator asked, heaving the closet door shut.

"I'm not sure what my plans are," I admitted. "Here, take the spare keys."

Extracting the keys from a drawer in the television stand, I handed them over.

"Thanks."

"What are your plans," I asked, thinking I may want to tag along.

"First, I'll hit up Alta and see if I can get my hosting job back and then I need to stop by my apartment."

"You really think they held your job all this time?"

"No, but I'm better at it than anyone, they'd be insane not to take me back and give the new person the boot."

The Animator left in a hurry, all too ready to resume his life. I was left alone...with the business card. It was nearly impossible to resist sending a text, and the Animator was right, this was the setup to the perfect story. What are the odds of anyone else ever giving me their business card through a cab window without it being solicitation?

Retrieving my phone, I tried to construct the perfect sentence in my head. Several starts and stops later, I sent my message, *Do you always pick up guys on the street? -Ryan.* It was slightly offensive, presumptuous and a little bit funny. Things I consider myself to be, for the most part.

Sending a text message can be like sending a tiny little missile that turns around and explodes in your face. If the other person doesn't respond right away it can drive you mad. My mind began running through all of the psychotic scenarios it can muster: The guy wasn't really interested, maybe he was drunk when he gave me his card, he's a man whore that just likes attention, he's forgotten he gave me the card, he gives out so many cards he can't recall who this might be...and the list goes on.

As I was preparing to throw myself from the fire escape and admit defeat, of course blaming the Animator for sticking me in this situation, the phone lit up. Swiping a finger over the glass to open the message, *Only when they're attractive.* Good thing he was on the other end of the phone and not in front of me, I could feel my face burn red. Compliments made me nervous and uncomfortable.

The conversation progressed and we got to know a little about each other, or as much as you can learn when playing twenty text questions. This was the safest way to meet people and also the most dangerous. You can be anyone you want, but can't be sure the person on the other end is giving you any sort of truth.

A few hours passed and we agreed a date was in order. It was somewhat of a big deal for me; I hadn't been on an actual date in longer than I cared to remember. Other than a few hookups, that wouldn't qualify as dates, even in the loosest of terms, I'd pretty much kept to myself the last year.

A few hours later the Animator returned from his mission to reclaim a job abandoned and apartment surrendered.

"How'd it go?" I asked, settled on the sofa with a beer and my laptop.

"Well. Really well."

"They gave you your job back? Actually, they gave me a management position."

"Congrats."

"But it gets better."

"Oh?" Now I was intrigued, what could possibly be better than getting a job the instant you ask for it?

"I stopped by my apartment to talk with the tenant."

"They're willing to vacate?"

"Not exactly," the Animator answered, a devious look coming over his face.

"What then?" If the person wouldn't leave, what was the good news?

"We had sex and we're going on a date later!"

This was the most unexpected thing that could have come from his mouth. He was either the smoothest guy on Earth or incredibly lucky.

"That's exactly the reaction I was expecting."

"How did you ever end up having sex?"

"Well, for starters, I pulled his pants *down*-"

"Okay, not what I meant."

"It just happened. I was explaining how I needed him to move out at the end of the month. He didn't argue, next thing I knew his hands were in my pants and his head was bobbing up and down in my lap."

"So, he just sucked you off and accepted you tossing him out?" Something was off about this tenant; no one was this understanding, or friendly.

"Actually, we never finished the discussion. I'll have to bring it up at dinner."

"Fun conversation. *I really like the way you blow me, now get out of my apartment.* You'll sound like a straight guy."

"I am trying to be more butch," the Animator, mocked my comment. "And if all else fails, we can fool around again, he gives great head."

The Animator, though a tad slutty at the moment, did inspire me to write, or at least to ponder the casual sex concept. Tomorrow, I would go on a date with someone that picked me up on a street corner, would that parlay into casual sex? Or would this backseat Romeo turn out to be something more?

3. Adult

First dates are always nerve-racking, which is why I was trading contacts for glasses tonight. Eyeglasses had become a sort of security blanket that could rest on my nose without anyone knowing they were helping to hide my insecurity. During the embarrassingly short tour to promote my last book, I'd been forced to speak in front of several crowds, my least favorite activity. What I took from the experience was the way people reacted to me with glasses and without. With glasses on, people were generally friendly and inquisitive about my work, without glasses there were fewer questions and no one wanted to talk to me by the end of the night.

The idea that glasses make me more approachable was about to be tested as I wore them on my date with Leo. We agreed to meet at Sofia Wine Bar, a Midtown restaurant roughly between our apartments. More important, it was just off the 6 train, making it a short and easy escape home if things went horribly wrong.

Rent (minus) Control

As a Virgo, I'm compulsively early to engagements, mainly to appease my mind and avoid the stress of walking in late. Twenty minutes early, I sat on the neighboring building's stoop; the restaurant was small and filled to capacity. I could have waited at the bar, but in a place this *quaint* you're begging for stares.

Eight o'clock came and went, minutes ticking by as I grew less patient. Being an early arriver, I expect people to be on time, being forced to wait made me insane. Not to mention I was sitting outside, probably looking to passersby like a nicely dressed hobo. A few more minutes and a text message arrived, a quick apology blaming traffic for the delay, a lame but indisputable excuse.

Shortly after the message appeared on my phone a black car pulled up to the curb. Out stepped my backseat romancer, looking better than I remembered from our brief encounter.

"Sorry for being late," Leo said, leaning in to kiss my check.

"It's fine," I replied, surprised by the forward greeting.

One thing I'd never fully become accustom to was the standard East Coast greeting, kissing on the cheek. Invading my personal space was reserved for the strangers and perverts that rode the train alongside me, when it came to public affairs, I would grit my teeth and bear it; though it felt like torture and pushed way beyond my comfort zone. We're not European for God's sake.

"Shall we go in?"

I nodded, following Leo up the steps of Sofia. Passing through the black door adorned with small panes of glass, the entire restaurant became visible. From the street all that could be seen was the table jammed into the front window, truly meant for two, four people had managed to cram around the small piece of wood to enjoy an intimate evening.

Candles lit the restaurant with a romantic, almost sinister, orange glow that flickered over the faces at each table composed of couples deep in conversation.

"Do you want to grab a table or sit at the bar?"

"Let's sit at the bar if there's room," I said, peering over the rim of my glasses.

Three staff members were operating the restaurant from what I could tell. All of which appeared to be overwhelmed, the host passing by us as we pushed our way between chairs to the two empty seats at the end of the bar. Immediately it became clear why these seats were available. Each time the waiter or host passed by, they rammed into my chair back, jolting me forward.

"Do you know what you'd like?" asked the bartender...the incredibly attractive bartender. His exposed arms and neck were covered in tattoos; he was the kind of guy that would probably screw you and sneak out while you were sleeping, an exciting prospect.

"Can I get a glass of the Sauvignon Blanc? Do you know what you want?"

Seeing as this was a wine bar, it only felt appropriate to play along.

"I'll have the same."

"Anything to eat?" asked the bartender, holding the menus up like a photograph, his knuckles reading, *LOVE THIS*.

Leo looked to me for the response.

"I'm set for now. Thanks."

The bartender served our drinks, rushing up and down the bar to ensure the other patrons were taken care of as well. As Leo would glance away I found myself looking back to the bartender, as if I was daring him to catch me staring. There wasn't a reason for this, other than I liked what I couldn't have. Moments like this reminded me of my ex, the Devil, making me feel slightly bad and incredibly whore-ish.

"So, what do you do for work?" Leo asked, diving into the prescribed first date questions.

"I'm a writer." If only he would allow this answer to suffice.

"What do you write?"

"I blog and do some copywriting work, nothing special." It was my intent to not reveal the truth about my books.

Generally, when people discovered I wrote about my life, they walked away or became incredibly awkward. Worried their actions would end up in print. Which was a safe assumption.

"That's cool. I work in fashion design."

"Nice," I replied, sipping at my wine. For reasons unknown I was more nervous than usual, suddenly having nothing to talk about.

"Tell me about yourself."

Was it too late to abandon ship and end the date? Though I love to hear myself talk as much as any other self-absorbed person, I didn't want to get into the details of my life. My mouth became unusually dry, like I was chewing chalk.

"I grew up out West, have a brother and a sister, parents, the usual. What about you?"

"I grew up in Texas."

"Where are your cowboy boots and hat?"

"They take them away when you arrive at LaGuardia," Leo laughed. "Where out West are you from?"

"Utah," I reluctantly admitted.

"Oh, are you Mormon?"

"I'm not. Part of my dad's family is, my mom's family isn't really any religion that I know of."

"You don't know their religion?"

"No, I really don't know them in general."

There was a pause as I downed the remaining wine in my shallow glass.

"Can I get you another?" The bartender had perfect timing.

"Actually, can I get the IPA?" Screw being fancy for a date, I needed a beer if we were going to discuss family affairs.

"I guess you're not polygamist then."

"No, but we could have been."

"What do you mean?" Leo had a baffled look on his tan face.

"My parents have been divorced my entire life. Between the two of them I've had enough stepparents that we could've been polygamists, or at least started a harem of some sort."

A blank look said that Leo wasn't ready for my cynical sense of humor. For this reason I pulled back on being myself, keeping the jokes to a minimum and trying to stay on my best behavior.

We finished another round of drinks, the conversation staying light with a few laughs signaling that we were moving in the right direction.

"It's getting late and I need to be up early tomorrow," Leo said, rising from his place at the mahogany bar.

This was the type of quick night ending exclamation that either meant he was desperate to flee and get away from me, or he was responsible and wanted to ensure he didn't look hung-over in the morning. It was impossible to tell and allowed the suspicious mind to run wild with theories.

"That's probably a good idea," I said, finishing my drink and following Leo out the door.

"This was fun," he said, making me wonder if this was an official blow off. "We should hang out again." Now I was certain this was a blow off.

"Sure," I said, knowing it was unlikely that I'd ever see or hear from Leo again.

"Are you taking a cab?"

"I'm going to hop on the train, it's faster."

"Okay, well, I'm going to grab a cab, but we'll talk soon," Leo said, leaning in for a goodnight peck.

Hailing a cab, he was whisked away into the night.

Once home, the Animator was sprawled out on the sofa, enjoying a glass of something red.

"How was the cab driver date?"

"He's not a cab driver," I grimaced. "It was good...I think."

"What do you mean, you think?" asked the Animator, making room on the beckoning sofa for me to slouch by his feet.

"Everything went well, but I was so nervous I couldn't really be myself, you know how scary that can be."

"Yes, you are five feet and nine inches of true terror."

I provided the obligatory smirk.

"Oh, some Emily woman called."

"My editor?"

Folding the page of his book back to save his place, the Animator shuffled back through the pages, withdrawing a blue Post-it. Scribbled in barely legible red ink was an address in New Jersey along with Saturday's date and 4:00 P.M.

"What is this?" I asked, the message too short to be clear.

"She wants you to do a book signing."

"Really?"

The Animator gave a nod, having returned to his book and losing interest in my antic free evening.

"Did she say anything else?"

"No, just said to make sure you show up."

That definitely sounded like Emily. It had been over a year since she paraded me out in front of a crowd for an event. The last signing didn't go as planned, ending with me knocking over an enormous tower of books...that weren't even mine. It was hard to say if Emily or I had been more embarrassed. This was a bold move on her part...or desperate.

4. Fear

Saturday morning arrived along with the bus ticket Emily purchased for my trip to the Garden State Plaza. Not only was she cheap, any author travel coming out of her budget, but also she was evil, forcing me to ride a Chinatown bus.

It had been years since I'd been on one of the third-world Chinatown buses. Arriving late, I was the last person on the bus, meaning I had no choice but to take the only open seat. There was a reason this particular seat was available, the neighboring passenger was so robust his gut burst over the armrest. Squeezing myself into the ragged seat, the warmth of my neighbor's doughy flesh was felt over the left portion of my body.

The bus jolting forward, a squeal coming from the engine as we began to move. Trying to distract myself from the unwanted and unavoidable skin-to-skin contact, I examined the surroundings. The bare plastic of the floor was exposed, the carpet removed, only small tufts left around screws that held down the edges of the raised rubber aisle. Crumbs of food, dirt and a liquid that looked to be seeping from the toilet in the rear covered the black floor, encouraging me to keep my bag securely on my lap.

The other passengers were a sight to behold, a man across the aisle eating from a tinfoil container. Whatever it was smelled like death. A woman a few rows up could be clearly heard, but not fully understood, as she yelled at what I assumed to be her baby-daddy on the phone. A child screamed from somewhere near the front of the bus, I hadn't noticed children while boarding. This was some sort of conspiracy between parents and their children; keep quiet until you're on the bus, plane or train and then go fucking ballistic once everyone is trapped.

Plugging in the earbuds of my phone, I hoped to find relief in the loud music that would potentially deafen me. While searching for a song with a loud beat, the bus hit an enormous pothole, my seat fully reclining with force onto the knees of the passenger behind me. Seconds later thrusting back to the stationary position. Maybe it wasn't just my whale-sized neighbor encouraging people to skip this seat. Another pothole and there I was laying in some girl's lap.

"Move ya fuckin' seat," screeched the female behind me, her long pink fingernail waving in the air as if she had gone into drag queen defense mode.

"It's not like I want to be on top of you," I grumbled back, leaning forward to remove the pressure that allowed the seat to flail uncontrollably at every bump in the road.

An hour and too many minutes later we arrived at the mall. My back was sore from lurching forward for so long, the girl behind me one of the first to stand up and rush to the front of the bus, as if we were being held prisoner and only a few inmates would be allowed to leave. I resisted the urge to stick my foot and trip her, but it was more the stickiness of the floor slowing my reflexes than me being polite.

Exiting the bus, clutching a bag with a few signed books to my chest, I made eye contact with Emily who was leaning against a ZipCar.

"Please tell me you didn't drive here."

"Of course, darling." There was that fake British accent I hated.

"Why the hell did you make me ride the bus?" Emily was generally infuriating, but this topped this list of her asshole moves.

"It keeps you humble. I also didn't want to force conversation for an hour."

"I hate you so much right now."

"Oh darling, you'll live."

"A man sat on me for an hour."

"Is that what that smell is?" Emily asked, leading us toward the mall's entrance.

"No, that's probably the fried chicken or gaflaka-somethin' that everyone and their Jewish mother was eating on the bus."

"I enjoy you all wound up like this, but save it for a book."

As Emily brushed off my bitter attitude we arrived at Barnes & Noble. Five small tables had been setup near the front of the store, each supporting a stack of books and a hungry author with a pen positioned behind, ready to sell their dignity.

"What is this?"

"A signing," Emily replied with a curt smile.

"Why are there other people here?"

"It's a new author event."

"I'm not a new author."

"You may as well be with the dismal book sales you're pulling in."

It was like Emily had set out to piss me off today. She was going to greater lengths than ever before to be a bitch.

"You're here," Emily directed me to the table stacked with books, the recognizable grey Manhattan skyline on the cover. "I'm going to hunt down the tart we need to check in with, be back."

Sitting behind the table, I pulled from my bag a pen and notepad. I was committed to sitting in this hard metal chair for the next four hours. Meaning I may as well jot down a few ideas as I wait for the occasional lost shopper to stop and ask me for directions.

"Hi, I'm Jon Soul, how are you?"

"Good thanks," I glanced up; the dark-haired man from the next table was hovering above.

"*Rent minus Control*, what's it about, housing codes?"

"No," I answered, is that what people think when they read the title? No wonder books aren't selling. "It follows my life in New York. What's-" I glanced around him to see his book's title. "*The Quest*, about?"

"The journey of two siblings into a magical world where they fight for good."

"Like Harry Potter?" Ask if my book was about housing codes and I'll be sure to get you back.

"No, this is much more original."

"That's good, you're going to have to be incredibly original to make a mark on the world of science-fiction now that Harry Potter dominates."

That was enough to send Mr. Soul away. There was something about authors, anytime two got together it became a verbal battle to prove which has the better book. Every writer thinks their work is the best, it's a pointless argument no one can win.

Back to my notepad, I put a few ideas down that could potentially make their way into a new book or at least a blog post. I was fixating on my date with Leo from earlier in the week. A perfectly normal date, but he hadn't sent a follow up text, validating my initial suspicion that no second date was going to take place.

As quickly as she had abandoned me, Emily reappeared, grasping a frail and frantic woman by the arm.

"This is Lydia, the coordinator of today's event," Emily announced.

I stood to shake her hand and offer a simple, 'hello.'

"Hi Robert, so nice to meet you. Do you have everything you need?" Lydia asked, a mousey girl with long, scraggly brown hair and a complexion so pale she rivaled me for whitest person in Jersey.

"I'm great."

"If you need anything don't hesitate to ask. The cafe in the back will also provide you any drinks or pastries you'd like, just let them know you're one of our authors."

"Will do," I said, nodding politely.

Always the center of attention, Emily grabbed Lydia by the shoulder and turned away from me, her black hair concealing her mouth but not muffling the words.

"What was that about going '*up*'?" I asked, distinctly hearing something about a time and me.

"You'll be the second reading of the night, right around 7:30," Lydia smiled, taking her cue to escape Emily's clutches.

"I didn't agree to do a reading."

"I did. Readings interest patrons and sell books."

"You know I'm terrible in front of crowds."

"I do, which is why you need to do this. You have to be comfortable speaking in public. Even more important, you must be comfortable reading your own stories allowed."

"No way, I'm not getting up in front of a crowd, last time was disastrous."

"Let me put this nicely," Emily curled her painted red lips into a sort of smile. "You will get on that stage and read the excerpt I've selected."

"And if I don't?"

"That's not an option. Your book has barely sold five thousand copies, that's nothing. I'm doing everything I can to keep this sinking ship of yours afloat. The least you can do is get your ass on the stage and read the shit I'm peddling."

"Well, when you put it so nicely."

"I've marked what I want you to read," Emily said, handing me a copy of my book, a page folded down, text highlighted in blue.

"Seriously?"

"It's the juiciest part."

"I can't get up there and read about getting handcuffed and screwed," I whispered, hoping the other authors couldn't hear.

"You have to, think of it as being your very own, Fifty Shades of Gay."

Emily abandoned me once more to stalk poor Lydia who was probably hiding in her office at this point. I read and reread the portion I was being forced to publicly share. There's something about writing dirty things that is liberating when you're in front of a computer all alone. But when it comes to sharing the stories in front of a group of strangers it quickly turns into a nightmare equivalent to going to school naked in a dream.

The clock ticked forward with feverish speed, my chest tightening, palms sweating and words twisting into unintelligible sentences at the few passersby that made to stop and ask about my work. And then it was time to climb the single step and sit in front of the fifteen people that felt like five hundred.

Clearing my throat, I began,

"Sitting down beside London on his pullout bed, my energy began to fade as the alcohol fully enveloped my body. Again he took my hand, but this time the gesture was followed by a click, click, click. Before my eyes could focus on what was happening, London thrust me back, flipping me over and making another click, click, click. Struggling to free myself, I realized he'd handcuffed me. Heart racing, I did my best to turn over, London taking charge and forcing my face into the pillows."

I could feel the sweat on my forehead beginning to bead, this was the most humiliating moment of my life and it was about to get worse. A hard swallow and I forced myself through the words that described London pulling down my pants and thrusting himself inside without warning. Tripping on my tongue, I could see a few disgusted onlookers, others intrigued by the sexual encounter. At the end of an eternity in the spotlight there was a very light clap from the audience as I shuffled off the stage with my dignity shoved up inside of me like London's penis.

"I enjoyed your reading," said a tall man as I did my best to scurry away unnoticed.

"Thanks. I feel like drinking myself stupid after that."

"I'm Paul."

"Ryan," I replied, shaking the outstretched hand.

"I know," he said, holding up a copy of my book.

"Right."

"Can I buy you that drink?"

Desperate to escape and not ready to climb back on the bus from hell, I agreed to Paul's offer.

"I just need to do one thing first," I said, scuttling over to my table and signing the copies that remained. "Ok, good to go."

Leaving the bookstore I noticed Emily coming up from the back, I hastened my step to get us away before she could force me into some other humiliating act.

5. Ho-Tales

During our car ride to the nearest watering hole, which turned out to be a Chili's, truly the finest Paramus has to offer, I learned Paul is a pilot for emergency services. He was tall, had dark wavy hair, piercing blue eyes, a nice build and he saved lives, what was secretly wrong with him?

"Two for dinner?" asked the hostess as we entered the nearly vacant restaurant.

"Can we sit at the bar?" I asked.

Her disappointed look said yes as she returned attention to her iPhone.

The bartender, decked out in an array of embarrassing pins he was forced to wear, quickly serviced our order and left us to converse with an easy-looking waitress in a similar uniform.

"So, Paul the Pilot, what do you do other than save lives and pick up guys at bookstores?" I asked, washing away the night with the assistance of alcohol.

"I'm a pianist."

"Really?"

"Yep," he was as uncomfortable talking about himself as I was, avoiding eye contact as I questioned him.

"Professionally?"

"Not so much these days. I used to perform with an orchestra, but now I work on pieces and sell them when I can."

"That's impressive."

"I guess. What about you, do you do anything along with writing?"

"Not really. It's sort of taken over my life."

"That's the dream, right?"

"Yeah, I'm not complaining."

"Was the portion you read true?"

Oh God, now he wanted to know if I was as big a slut as it sounded when I was getting verbally penetrated on stage.

"Yes," I admitted through gulps of room temperature beer.

"Want another round?" Paul the Pilot asked, noticing I drained the stout mug.

"Yes, please. I'm especially parched tonight."

A few more rounds and the question arose,

"Do you live around here?"

"I live in the city. I guess I should be finding a train or bus to get me home; it's starting to get late.

"My hotel is nearby if you'd like to stay."

"I thought you lived here?" I asked, knowing he told me earlier that he had a house somewhere in Jersey.

"I'm farther South, I was up here visiting family."

"They won't let you stay in the house?"

"They will, it's just easier to take cute boys home when I have a hotel and privacy."

"You're in the closet?" An unappealing prospect.

"No, I'm just not comfortable having sex in my parents' house."

"You think we'll be having sex?"

"I'm pretty sure we will."

"That's awfully cocky of you."

Grabbing my hand and running it over his pants, either Paul the Pilot had the longest cell phone made since the 1980's or he had a good reason for being so cocky.

Exiting the restaurant and locating the car, Paul the Pilot unlocked my door opening it for me like a gentleman. As I made to enter he pinned me against the rear door, leaning down for a kiss, grasping the back of my neck to ensure there could be no resistance. Pulling away, I bit at my lip, Paul's eyes locking on mine, a short smile and he made for the driver's side of the car.

Paul the Pilot drove us to his hotel, neither of us speaking on the way. It was a standard roadside Hilton, nothing spectacular that would suggest the Pilot was planning on a hookup. Which made me feel less like a hooker now that I was committed to performing the act.

Upstairs, I was surprised when a bottle of wine was pulled from a suitcase. Accepting a glass, I hoped there was a roofie or something in the red juice that would calm my nerves. Pacing slowly around the room I took in the generic surroundings. The light yellow wallpaper, brown Berber carpet, a sad wood panel desk, bed and dresser set. Everything was cheap, manufactured crap that fit any hotel decor.

"Can I get you anything else?" Paul the Pilot asked.

I turned to see him come around the corner from the bathroom, shirt off and muscled body on display. Shaking my head and sipping at the wine, I didn't know what to say, but so far the show was worth watching.

Moving in, the Pilot took the glass from my hands, placing it on the desk next to his glass that had never been filled. Grabbing at the hem of my shirt, he pulled it over my head, running his eyes over my body. The Pilot's massive hands nearly touched when he placed them around my waist, moving us toward the bed. In a smooth movement, the Pilot laid me on my back, his mouth moving from mine down my neck, his hands running up my inner thigh, searching for a zipper.

"Buttons?" Paul the Pilot asked, his fingers tugging at the resistant pants.

"I like to provide a challenge."

The Pilot's tongue traced over my chest, fixating on my stomach as his hands worked to unfasten the buttons that held my pants in place. As the buttons released I could feel the Pilot's energy, my pants and black underwear I had been wise to wear, slipping off as he kneeled. In a sudden moment of self-satisfaction I was happy to have taken the time the night before to groom myself from head to toe.

A deep breath escaped as the Pilot consumed me in a single movement, his head bobbing slowly as my fingers found his hair, grasping as he continued, his head twisting, the sensation forcing me to let out a moan. I closed my eyes, the Pilot's hands moving over my chest squeezing as he bore down on me. He paused for a moment, retracting as he searched for something in a bag on the floor.

The familiar sound of a crinkling condom wrapper came as the Pilot rose from his knees, his pants dropping as he did so. I was stunned, he felt big through jeans, but now that we were face to cock, it was definitely the biggest one I'd seen. I wished at this moment the glass of wine was within arm's reach. All I could think was that this was going to hurt.

Tearing open the gold wrapper, the Pilot groaned as he rolled the sticky round rubber over himself, it was clearly a bit too small, only stretching halfway down the shaft when fully unfurled. Leaning back into me our lips reconnected, the Pilot positioning his arm behind my knee and penetrating the space between my body and the comforter, teasing me as his tongue moved in and out of shallow kisses.

Hair brushing my face as the Pilot looked down, grasping himself with a free hand, he pulled up and pressed forward, this time penetrating more than the comforter. A deep breath, clenched eyes and a moan all uncontrollably releasing.

"You ok?" the Pilot asked, stopping mid-thrust.

I nodded, unable to speak; it felt like the wind had been knocked from me. Paul the Pilot's slow pace began to gain momentum as my body relaxed, his open palm pressing down against my chest, sweat beginning to form on his chest and brow. Reaching down, with a smooth stroke he made sure I was having a good time, my lack of sounds not providing the encouragement he was probably used to receiving.

The Pilot didn't lose speed, putting his arm around my back and pulling me forward, his height still forcing him to lean into the bed as he was partially crouched on the floor. Holding me against his chest, he groaned loudly, his movements becoming long and slow as he came. Pulling back slowly, he removed the condom, tossing it into the bedside trash bin for a maid to find, focusing again on me.

I grabbed his hand to stop him.

"I'll never finish."
"I'm in no rush."
"It's really ok. I need to get back to the train anyway."

A moment in the bathroom to cleanup and get my clothes on and I was ready to go. No one could ever classify me as a power bottom. As far as really big dicks were concerned, the moment they caused pain I was done.

"Can I drive you to the train?"

"Sure," I said, not wanting to refuse and force myself to wander in the dark, likely to get raped or murdered.

Locating the nearest Jersey Transit station, Paul the Pilot gave me a kiss and let me go on my way with an exchange of numbers. The train was quick to arrive, rescuing me from my Jersey adventure and catapulting me back to reality.

6. Brunch

None of my friends in the city had children, mainly because they were gay and/or single. Not to say that Business or one of the others couldn't adopt or find a surrogate, but none of my friends had made it far enough in a relationship for children to become a topic of discussion. All except for one.

Lacee and I had lived together in Brooklyn where we enjoyed white trash dinners by candlelight, due to the buildings lack of power at times, and property damaging joyrides to and from IKEA, due to our horrific driving skills. Lacee and her on-again-off-again boyfriend, Brad, moved in together when an accidental pregnancy forced them to decide where the relationship was headed. This isn't to say they ran off to the Bronx and lived a fairytale life, no, things are just as painful for them, probably more so now that they have two children.

Lacee and I found it harder and harder to spend time together with my general dislike of children, and Brad's ability to vanish when he was supposed to be babysitting. But somehow the planets aligned and the babysitting gods smiled on us, allowing Lacee to break free of parental bondage for brunch at Midnight Blue around the corner from my place. It was a two level restaurant with an amazing brunch. Sadly, in the evening it turned into a dance club filled with guidos standing on the second floor balcony hooting at the women walking past.

Knowing Lacee would be excited to see the long-lost Animator, I brought him along, coaxing him with the promise of bottomless mimosas. Arriving a few minutes early, the restaurant was nearly empty, one couple sitting at the bar watching sports on the massive screen surrounded by bottles of booze. The waitress sat the Animator and I in the front windows, both still closed, the morning air particularly chilly for early summer.

Midnight Blue was doomed from the moment it opened a few months earlier. Construction of the Second Avenue Subway blocked the street view of their sign, encouraging people to walk on the opposite side of the avenue to avoid the dust, noise and construction workers. It wasn't a terrible place, the interior was supposed to look Mediterranean, I think. Blue and yellow tiles decorated the lower half of the walls and bar, the remainder painted a deep blue with poorly copied constellation patterns. It was cute.

As our second round of mimosas arrived, Lacee entered, cheeks pink from the air and out of breath from rushing.

"Animator!" Lacee squealed.

We rose, the Animator sipping his drink, providing a one-armed hug.

"Sorry for being late. Brad tried to get out of watching the kids."

"No problem, you're here now," I said, handing Lacee a brunch menu.

"But oh my god, Mator Mator, what are you doing here?" Lacee asked, the intuitive waitress arriving with a mimosa for the newest guest.

"I moved back."

"Yay! Did you get a new job in the city?"

"I got my old job back. Now I'm just working on getting my apartment back."

"What do you mean, get your apartment back?" Lacee asked, sipping at her drink, a facial spasm revealing the strength of the cheap vodka being used.

"I sublet it when I moved. I just have to wait until the end of the month to kick the guy out."

"Which will be even more difficult now that you're sleeping with him," I added.

"I'm confused. How are you sleeping with your tenant?"

"It just happened when I went over to evict him. Then we had dinner and fooled around the other night. No big deal."

"He's never going to leave if you keep sleeping with him."

"It's hard to stop. He has a very talented mouth," the Animator shared, relishing in his conquest. "And you can't judge, you slept with a stranger during your book signing."

"You had a book signing?" Lacee asked, excited at the prospect of our gossip being spread among others.

"Ok, you missed the best part of that statement," added the Animator.

"Share, who did you sleep with?"

"This guy that was at the signing."

"That's all?" Lacee asked, her face falling flat with disappointment.

"Tell her the best part."

"He had the biggest penis I've ever seen."

"How big?"

"It was like a third arm. My ass is still sore. I need one of those little ass pillows."

"Wow, that's scary."

"It gave me flashbacks to when you slept with the security guy in our old apartment. Remember how you felt the next day?"

"That was worse than giving birth...*twice.*"

Lacee's bag began vibrating below the table, retrieving the massive mommy purse, she searched for her phone. Out came a bottle, tampons, pacifier and to my surprise condoms.

"You carry condoms?" I asked, surprised they were regular size. I'd assumed Brad was scary big like many of the men Lacee landed.

"I'm not getting pregnant again. This way I always have one."

"You should have started carrying those years ago," quipped the Animator.

"Truth. Brad has super sperm; he can get me pregnant just by looking at me. Sorry, hold on one sec." Lacee located the buzzing phone. "Hello...I'm at brunch, what do you want...No...No."

"Everything ok?" I asked, Lacee tossing the phone back in her purse and dropping it under her chair.

"Fine, Brad's just being a douche bag."

"Cheers to the douche bags."

Eventually food arrived at the table, breakfast at one in the afternoon, just the way civilized society intended. Our rants on bad dates, hookups and home issues continued. That was until a familiar face appeared in the restaurant with a double stroller.

"What are you doing here?" Lacee asked as Brad rolled over to our table with her infant and toddler in tow.

"I told you I need to pick up a shift at work."

"You couldn't wait until I got home?"

"You hung up on me. I tried to wait."

"Hi Brad," I interjected, hoping to diffuse some of the rising tension.

"Hey, guys. Anyway, I've got to go, the diaper bag has a couple changes in it and formula so you don't have to go home right away."

"Thanks. Thanks a lot," Lacee grumbled.

Brad exited the restaurant as quickly as he'd appeared, abandoning the children with a table of terrified gays and one pissed off mommy.

"Sorry, I didn't know he would show up like that."

"Things seem more tense than usual with you two," I said, poking at the eggs on my plate.

"No...l don't know. I think he's banging some Chinese slut at work."

"This is the conversation I'm here for," said the Animator, waving an empty glass at the waitress in hopes of receiving a refill. "Tell us all about China."

"I don't know if anything is going on between them, but they text each other every day."

"If he lets you see his messages, that's a good sign," I added, though skeptical of what it really meant.

"Brad doesn't know I've been reading his messages. I figured out his phone's passcode."

"That's dangerous," remarked the Animator, impatiently awaiting his drink.

"I know I shouldn't be looking, but he won't discuss her if I bring up the topic. That makes me think there's something to hide."

"It's possible. Is that why he's picking up extra shifts?" I asked.

"I think so. I know she works on Saturday afternoons. Brad works the night shift so their schedules don't overlap unless he takes someone else's shift."

Now I was in agreement with Lacee that her boyfriend was probably sleeping with China. As much as we all love money, who in their right mind is going to volunteer to work an eight hour day shift followed by an eight hour night shift at the Apple store? Not to mention it's the Fifth Avenue store where there is a nonstop crowd, tons of tourists and other crazy people all hoping to take a photo in or around the glass cube. It's a terrifying place.

"Do you guys think I should say something?" Lacee asked, bouncing her kid on one knee to keep him from crying.

"I don't know, it's probably just going to turn into a fight."

"Say something. If you don't ask, you'll never know," said the Animator, now breaching the line of sobriety. "Even better, you should wipeout his phone's data and then see whose number he adds back first. If he adds the girl's number back right away he's probably sleeping with her."

"Yeah, but he'll know I did something if his phone is wiped out."

"That's not true. Do you have his account login for the computer?"

"Yeah."

"Log in and delete it from there. He can assume you did something, but he'll have no way to prove it."

"Maybe."

"Or you could just march down to Apple and confront China. Go all Jerry Springer on her. She might spill her guts." I shouldn't encourage bad behavior, but it was the kind of scene that would be great in my new book.

"I better go, Kaymen is getting fussy."

Lacee rose from the table, positioning her baby back in the stroller, her daughter sleeping in the back seat. With a wave goodbye, she huffed out of the restaurant and up the street toward the subway.

"She's nicer than me, I would have pitched a fit if someone dumped their kids on me."

"They are hers, but I agree, I'd be pissed if my baby daddy pulled that stunt," I said, finishing off my mimosa. "Do you think he's cheating?"

"Probably, he's a guy. Guys are whores."

It was hard giving advice on how to approach the situation. The Animator and I had both been cheated on at different points, making us less forgiving than some others. I couldn't be sure of how Lacee was going to deal with the issue, but I made a mental note to check in on things in case a juicy storyline developed.

7. Mommy

My short couch did not play host to the lengthy Animator for long. Another week of sleeping with the morally loose tenant and he was back in his apartment. There was a small hitch in the original plan, the tenant technically left, or the label left, and he stayed in the apartment, becoming the boyfriend. I'd yet to meet the guy, but it seemed that someone was taking advantage of the situation, it just wasn't possible to tell who.

The vacant sofa came at the perfect time; my mom was coming to town for the Fourth of July. The timing made even better as she had recently ended a seven-year relationship and I needed someone to drink on the fire escape with as drunken fools stumbled around on the street in celebration. Our relationship is unconventional by typical mother-son standards, but I think that's a positive. We have the type of relationship I believe most parents wish they had with their children once they're adults.

Arriving by town car on a rainy morning, I buzzed her in; she'd visited New York enough times that there was no longer a need to meet at the airport.

"Hey, how was your flight?" I asked, greeting mom with a hug as she pulled her roller bag into the apartment.

"There were two little kids behind me that wouldn't shut up the entire flight. By the time we took off I was so wound up I couldn't fall asleep."

"So you've been up all night?"

"I just need a quick nap and then I'll be good to go."

"We're in no rush," I lied; ready to get our day underway.

"Have you gone for coffee yet?"

"No, I was waiting for you to get here."

"Would you mind getting me a chocolate mocha Frappuccino?"

"That's so bad for you."

"I don't give a shit. Make sure they also put whipped cream on it."

Obliging, I made my way over to Starbucks, ordering myself a skinny vanilla latte, and with a guilt-ridden tone my mother's chocolate decadence. I felt compelled to tell the barista the drink wasn't for me. I didn't want this kid thinking I was suddenly consuming mass amounts of sugar...not that he cared or paid any attention to what I was drinking. This was like when she asked me to grab cigarettes from the bodega below my apartment. I don't smoke, and not that the salesperson was interested, but I always told the cashier the smokes weren't for me. I'd rather they think I was buying them for a twelve year old.

One nap later, two coffees and we were out the door and ready to begin mom's vacation. It was tradition to begin each trip by walking over the Brooklyn Bridge. The first year I'd lived on the Upper East Side, I failed to mention we would be walking from Manhattan to Brooklyn. This didn't fly, as mom couldn't get the same skyline view while we walked. Not that Brooklyn doesn't have a unique skyline, but Manhattan has the better-known buildings, making for great photo-ops. Since that visit it was made clear that we walk from Brooklyn to Manhattan, no exceptions.

The 5 train to Fulton Street, a transfer to the A and we arrived at our destination, High Street. From this subway stop you could walk to the entrance of the bridge, located next to a diner I was fond of because a Russian waitress once told me I had beautiful blue eyes. I'm a sucker for all and any compliments as long as they are coming from someone who isn't sexually interested; it's also a great way to ensure repeat business when your industry is suffering from an over-saturated market.

A worn line of yellow paint divided the long stretch of concrete leading to the bridge. This was meant to give bicyclists and pedestrians their own pathways. Somehow, pedestrians always ended up in the bike lane and bicyclists wherever the hell they felt like. Each more annoyed by the other than anything else in the world. Bicyclists get a thrill from whizzing by dinging their little bells and shouting as if they have some authority.

I have a special kind of hatred for anyone that jumps on a bike and speeds around. All I want to do is grab a stick and toss it in their spokes, sending them head over handlebars into the concrete. I'd never done it, but thinking about it was exciting.

Eventually we made it, safely, to the bridge. You know you're officially crossing the threshold when the concrete ends and wood planks appear. As you walk farther along you see the cars on the deck below, honking and breaking as they rush around, and if you look with intent, you can see the water directly below the bridge and whatever boats may be passing at the moment. A little terrifying for those who prefer solid ground.

"Stand on the side so I can take a picture."

Mom pointed to a spot within the massive tangle of cables that suspended us over the water.

"I really don't want to get up there," I said, not comfortable with heights or the idea I could plummet backwards into oncoming traffic.

"Just do it, it'll take two seconds."

Rather than debate why I didn't want to take this or any photo, I hoisted myself onto the flat steel girder covered in several decades' worth of chipping paint.

"Pose. Grab the thick pole or something."

"I thought the goal was to keep your kids off the pole?"

"Smart-ass. Hold still."

"Do you want to grab a drink?" I asked, climbing down from the windy perch the moment the camera clicked.

"Sure."

"We could go to South Street Seaport, the Village bars or the Fat Black Pussycat."

"Let's do the Pussycat. I want to get a shirt since I forgot last time."

"Done."

Our walk concluded with shoving through the hundreds of tourists clogging our way and many vendors pedaling crap to feed their insatiable need to buy. Happy to be away from the crowd, I hailed a cab, sending us toward the Village. The Fat Black Pussycat was a find during Mom's previous visit. The name and the black neon cat sign with its giant martini glass drew us in.

The Pussycat had a dark decor that survived from the 1800's or possibly had been expertly recreated. It was a straight bar that was fun by day and an NYU tragedy by night. It was still early enough that the place would only have a few local drunks, us included. Finding a place at the bar we waited for the bartender to make her way over, busy in the corner with her glowing phone.

"This is bullshit," Mom said, annoyed at the slow service. "Where's our bartender from last time?"

"Maybe she's new."

"What can I get you?" asked the brunette bartender in an ill-fitting tank top, finally acknowledging us.

"Can we get a pitcher of Bud Light?" I asked, noting the special written in pink marker on the mirror behind the bar.

"Why's the cat not on?" Mom asked.

"What cat?" asked the bartender, perplexed by the non-alcohol related question.

"The cat. Up there," Mom pointed to a place between the door and the bar where a smaller version of the neon cat on the exterior of the building was perched.

"Oh, I didn't even know that was there," the bartender chuckled.

"You have to have the cat on, it's the whole reason we come here."

Unsure of how to answer the request, the bartender left an amber pitcher of beer, stepping away with an awkward smirk, returning to the phone that was plugged in near the register.

"Where's our guy from last time, he'd turn the sign on for me."

During our last visit, the bartender had not only been entertaining, but had given mom a complete tour of the bar, including the roped off area in the back even I've never seen. She did have a way of charming strangers. I'm convinced that she should own a gay bar, though I'd be jealous of the other gays vying for her attention.

"This beer is warm," Mom griped, sipping at the mug I'd poured from the pitcher provided us.

"We can ask for another."

"Let's just go, this isn't the Fat Black Pussycat I remember."

"You don't want to finish your beer?"

"It's piss warm, I'm not drinking it. Let's go back to the apartment and order food and get a twelve-pack."

"Okay," I muttered through gulps, trying to down my beer before we left. Cheap or not, I hate wasting a drink.

One of my favorite things about New York is the availability of mass transit and the numerous cabs clogging the streets. With a hail and a bumpy ride we were right back where we started. Even more convenient, the bodega carried mom's preferred beer, saving a walk to the store.

Before I'd even placed the beer in the fridge mom was out the window on the fire escape with a cigarette, people watching.

"Here," I offered a beer, climbing out the window to join in the festivities.

The holiday was still a day away, but it wasn't stopping people from getting into the spirit early. Dorrian's was a popular bar and restaurant directly across from my building. The place never failed to bring in a string of interesting characters. Over the past year alone I had been witness to a fist fight between a homeless man and a bar patron, seen a man put his foot through the glass door of the adjacent building and even caught a girl as she puked out the bar window.

Dorrian's had a long and interesting history, stemming back some fifty years. The most shocking moment came in the 80's when a preppy college guy took a drunk girl, raped and beat her in Central Park before leaving her for dead. At least that's

65

how the story was passed down to me from Mom. Though the crime was horrific, I did like living across from a story-generating establishment, for better or worse.

We were only halfway through the twelve-pack when a character appeared on the street. A robust man, dressed in jeans and a green t-shirt, clearly intoxicated from the way he was stumbling. A police van was parked on the street, the drunkard deciding it was a good idea, or possibly funny, to climb on the hood and pose like a pin-up girl. Whatever he was thinking, it was pure entertainment as he struck pose after pose for passing pedestrians. Where are this guy's friends?

The police appeared from the bodega, coffee in hand. To my surprise they laughed while trying to coax the drunken man off their vehicle. These two had to be the nicest cops in the city. Climbing on a cop car had to be one of the many things they could arrest you for, not to mention being so drunk that you're willing to do it right in front of a cop. A few more minutes of what looked to be polite persuasion and one of the officers was able to get the chubby bar patron down. We couldn't hear what they were saying, but it looked like the cop was asking if the guy was ok, based on his head tilt and the way he was holding the man's arm. This is the mannerism of a person faking interest.

A few more minutes and the man controlled himself enough for the officer to leave him standing on the sidewalk. The moment the van pulled away, our drunken friend pulled out something else. His penis. Standing behind the mailbox, which in his mind must have made him invisible to others on the street, the guy pulled out his junk and began peeing right there in broad daylight. The sexy van poses had us laughing, but now, Mom and I were in stitches, choking on our beers through teary eyes.

I've had enough drinks on occasion to pee on the street, in the subway and a number of other places, but I always attempt to find a dark corner. Through the grapevine I know the citation when caught is fifty dollars, more than I'm willing to pay for any physical release. With a jiggle and a zip, our friend's little friend was tucked back in his saggy jeans.

There were a handful of people on the street, no one taking notice of the urine soaked mailbox. Including the bouncer of a neighboring bar just a few feet away, stretching out a hand to shake. We shouted pleas of *'no'* from our position on the fire escape, but our cries went unheard. The entire man mess was the funniest thing I'd seen in a long time.

Made funnier when the guy attempted to hail a cab. Cabs would stop, realize how inebriated the guy was and speed away. This continued for several minutes, the guy stumbling into the middle of the street. Either he was going to get picked up or run down, determination. We lost sight of him as he became frustrated, wobbling up Second Avenue and out of view.

"Oh my god, that's the funniest thing."

"It must have been just for you. I've never seen anyone that crazy out here," I said, finishing my beer and crunching up the can.

Climbing back into the apartment, I fetched my phone a message waiting for my tipsy eyes. Being the obsessive personality that I am, after a few days passed without hearing from Leo, post-date, I'd assumed that was the end. Apparently, he ran on boy time and liked to wait the obligatory couple of days to torment and tease, highly effective.

"What are you doing?"

The message made me grin, even though I didn't want to be excited by the game of cat and mouse. Was it completely inappropriate to ditch my mom for a few hours? Probably, but it wasn't going to stop me. I agreed to stop by Leo's place later in the evening when things began winding down and Mom was ready for bed.

8. Petting

Mom and I have a friend-like relationship, but that doesn't mean she won't ask me fifty questions about where I'm going, who I'm with and when I'll be home...no matter how old I am. When I shared that I was planning to meet someone later in the evening, she was more than understanding, probably glad to get some alone time and relax for a moment after being drug all over the city. While providing some of the details, I did withhold that we were meeting at his apartment. That came off sluttier than the perception I aimed promote.

Making my way to Leo's, Murray Hill, apartment was less painful than originally thought. Paying twelve dollars for a cab wasn't worth the short ride, which meant the 6 Train was my best shot, even though it tripled travel time and hit every local stop along the way.

I wasn't entirely sure of what to expect, it was still a tad early for a booty call, but it wasn't a second date. It was some sort of in-between type of situation, this gave me a case of nerves, as I was unable to prepare. Holding down the buzzer, there was a short delay before the door made the deafening sound like something you'd hear in a prison psych ward. Climbing three long flights of stairs, I was winded by the time I reached the apartment. Less than ideal, now I was not only sweating from the heat of the train and walk over, but also I was out of breath from hiking this brick and mortar mountain.

A light tap and I waited for the door to pull back, but what came first was barking. I didn't realize there would be pets involved, most people have cats or no pets at all, many landlords are able to charge pet rent to punish a tenant's decision to have a furry companion.

"You made it."

"Yeah, though your stairs almost killed me."

"Come in, make yourself comfortable. Do you want a glass of wine?"

"Please," I really, really wanted the glass of wine. "What kind of dog is he...she?"

"She's a Shiba Inu," Leo responded, pulling a half empty wine bottle from the fridge.

"She's cute," I said, sitting in the armchair across from the dog now staring me down. "Does she bite?"

"No, she's just protective of her space."

Accepting the glass of wine, I moved over to the sofa where Leo positioned himself. Whether he said the dog was a biter, or not, I believe anything bigger than a Pug is going to try and rip my hand off.

"What are you watching?" I asked, taking note of a blonde woman bouncing across the screen.

"Real Housewives."

"Oh no, you're a reality TV watcher."

"It's funny."

"I feel like my brain cells die watching these shows."

While we watched I again felt a rush of nerves, what was going on in my head? Sipping at the wine, my mind was blank of any topics worth discussing, leaving us to watch in silence. Leo didn't seem to mind, but for me it was extremely uncomfortable to sit without saying a word.

Time passed slowly, checking my phone in between bathroom breaks and wondering if I should excuse myself to head home. That was until,

"You ready for bed?"

Was this an invitation to sleepover or was it a polite way of asking if I was ready to have sex?

"Sure." I was already there, no use in running off at this point.

The bedroom made me miss Brooklyn and apartments with space. Exposed brick with a no longer functioning fireplace, massive windows overlooking the street and even a second door in case a quick escape was needed. Was I more turned on by Leo or his apartment? Maybe I had been living in a studio for so long excess space gave me a hard-on.

Remaining semi-modest, underwear stayed on while initially slipping under the covers. Generally, guys were quick to make the first move. Leo was just lying there, when he asked if I was ready for bed did he truly mean sleep? It was starting to look that way.

In an effort to liven things up, my hand crept across the sheets, locating a furry torso. A hand clasped down on me, preventing any type of foreplay. Seconds later a light snore rang out, Leo was gone. Now it was just me in my head and the dog pacing around the foot of the bed.

Sneaking out was an option, but the bed was so creaky getting in, it would likely wake the dead if I attempted to move. Making matters worse, the apartment was eight hundred degrees. My pinned hand was sweating, adding to the discomfort of lying face down. Nothing to do but lay still until my racing mind finally gave up and relinquished to sleep. A true *fuck-my-life* moment.

Along with sunrise came the walk of shame, highlighted by the fact that my mom was going to be waiting for me at home. The sad part, there was no shame to be had, other than the fact that I looked a mess with my hair sticking in seven directions, nothing had happened. This was the virgin of hook-ups.

"How was your night?" I was greeted upon opening the apartment door.

"Not what I expected."

"I thought you were coming home last night."

"Me too. How about we grab breakfast and I'll give you the dirt?"

A quick shower, change of clothes and we were on our way. Diners are one of my favorite things about New York; they are everywhere and serve everything. No matter how newly established, every diner appears to be at least twenty years old from the decor. Vivand's around the corner was no exception, a long-standing diner with a deep and slender interior. Silver stools were pressed against the counter while small wooden booths lined the wall and offered patrons a retreat while watching the foot traffic outside.

"What happened with you and the boy last night?" Mom asked, her Coke and my coffee arriving.

"He just fell asleep, like two seconds in. What was the point of inviting me over?"

"He fell asleep in you?"

"God, no." I gulped. "Next to me. No sex."

"Maybe he wants something more."

"Then wouldn't it make more sense to ask me to dinner?" I grumbled, irritated by the whole situation, including my decision not to leave. "I think he changed his mind after I arrived and then was too nice to ask me to go."

"I don't think that's it. You're too pretty for him to lose interest. After all, you do look just like your mother."

"That's true. Thank god we're so self-centered. But enough about my drama, what's going on with you and Cort?"

"I threw him out."

A few weeks back Mom came across messages between her boyfriend of seven years and some random woman on Facebook. If we were less suspicious people it would be the kind of thing you overlook, but when you tell a stranger online you're looking forward to seeing them it becomes worth investigating.

"I asked him about Heidi."

"Is that her name?" I asked, finishing my coffee with a heavy gulp and hoping another would come quick.

"Heidi-Ho-Bag. I asked him if there's anything going on, he said no."

"Of course."

"But I found an email he sent her. Saying how much he *loves her and wants to be with her.*'"

"That's pretty damning evidence."

"It gets even better. I printed out the email and asked him about it."

"Oh god, what did he say?"

"I think he was stunned at first. Then he told me she was the '*love of his life.*'"

"Did you Lorena Bobbitt him?"

"I asked if he'd fucked her."

"Do you really want to know?"

"Hell yes, I want to know."

"Did he?"

"He didn't say yes or no, meaning he probably has or is planning to."

"Now what happens?"

"I'm going to take him to the cleaners. He can't screw around and think I'm going to walk away quietly."

Fortunately, Mom and her new ex lived in Utah. The state where you are common law married after living together for five minutes. Unless you're gay, then you're always living in sin by the religious standards of the state.

"Will you have to move?" I asked, worried Mom was about to become homeless.

"Eventually, my lawyer worked it out so he has to stay away until we finalize the details."

A lawyer? She wasn't wasting any time.

"You're welcome to move here."

"I know, but I don't want to crowd you."

"It would be fun...until I tried to do your laundry," I joked, having once removed Mom's clothing from the dryer only to let it wrinkle and nearly be slaughtered.

"Good thing there are all these dry cleaners."

"While on the topic of fun things, what would you like to do for the rest of your vacation?"

"I've about seen everything. I wouldn't mind relaxing while I'm here, ordering in and having some beers."

When I say that my mom lives in the country, she really lives in the country. In an area so remote it takes a little over three hours to drive there from the nearest regular city, if any city in Utah can measure up to any sort of normalization. Ferron, Utah is so small that Google Maps turns up nothing but hills, fields and the occasional cloud. It's the kind of place I go insane visiting, the Internet is slow and you lose cell service every time a heavy storm rolls in...which is constant in the winter.

The reason for ordering in was to indulge in all the delicious delivery that couldn't be had in Ferron. If nothing else, delivery would be the hardest thing to give up if I were to ever move outside the city.

"I have no objections to that plan."

Like two gluttons, Mom and I spent the next three days ordering everything GrubHub could provide. Pasta, grilled cheese, tacos, burgers, there was no limit to what my phone could bring us and we consumed it all. Right down to pizza and cheesecake from across the street...that we also had delivered, it was a vacation after all.

When it was time to put Mom in a cab back to JFK it was bittersweet as always. I was sad to see her go, but my body was glad that I'd be stopping the indulgent diet and going back to the gym. Which is exactly where I headed the moment her car was out of sight.

9. Nuts

Being a writer today is different from fifty years, even just ten, years ago. If you don't write the next 'Harry Potter' or a hit like 'Fifty Shades of Grey' you may as well resign to the fact that you'll always be under the radar. It's also highly probable that you'll spend more time telling people about your writing than they'll ever invest in reading your words.

Not giving into the delusions of my generation, that would be the idea that we all get to be, or deserve to be, famous, I remain cynical about writing. Books are something I create mainly for myself, and of course my editor, Emily, who is relentless about telling me to write smut, and the occasional reader that might discover me while surfing the web late at night. To ensure I don't end up living in a box on the street I do copyediting for nonprofits in the area and general blogging that allows advertisers to exploit readers with products no one needs.

That's not to say I wouldn't love to have a book be a best seller, allowing me to devout all the time I want to sitting in front of my laptop and not needing side jobs. Even the most cynical of us hold out a small bit of hope.

"Sorry I'm late."

I glanced up from my laptop, having lost myself in a thought bubble freshly spilled over the computer screen. Above me hovered Dimitri, whom I'd not seen since the birthday encounter where Shew caused unnecessary drama between him and his boyfriend.

"No worries, I was just putting a few ideas down," I smiled, closing the silver laptop and slipping it into my bag.

Dimitri worked as the head of IT for a mental hospital a few blocks from my apartment. This made it incredibly convenient for us to meet in the middle of the day for coffee. Even more convenient, the four Starbucks in between my place and his office, there was no lack of choice when it came to the multitude of formulaic coffee.

"How've you been?"
"Good. Really good. My mom was just in town."
"And you didn't bring her to meet us?" Dimitri asked, placing his tea on the table, pulling up a chair.
"We went out a little the first day she was here, but honestly, we just vegged out, watched fireworks from the window and had a good time on our own."
"Then I guess you're forgiven, but next time you have to bring her over for dinner or at least out for drinks."

"I'll warn you now, if you think I'm fun, she blows me out of the water."

"Even better. I'll bring my mom, they'll get along."

"Oh god, they'll be peas in a pod, we'll be in trouble."

"What's new in your dating world?" Dimitri asked, taking us off the subjects of mothers and onto the dirt we really wanted to discuss.

"Where to start. I had a non date-date with that guy, Leo. He invited me over to his place last week."

"How'd it go?"

"The reviews aren't in."

"Was the sex bad?"

"That's just it, there wasn't any sex. Not even a kiss."

"Then why'd he ask you to come over?"

"I've been asking myself the same question."

Apparently, Leo's behavior was as odd to my friends as it was to me.

"Are you going to see him again?"

"I don't know, probably." If nothing else I liked playing with fire, even when it wasn't burning. "What about you, did everything with your boy get fixed after Larry's birthday?"

"That was a disaster. We're still seeing each other but he's been acting weird ever since. I think Shew said more to him than I know and he's just not telling me."

"You told him it's all bullshit, right?"

"Yeah, and he says he knows, but I still think he believes the lies."

The funny thing about a lie, even a small lie, has the ability to grow out of control in someone's mind and ruin everything. To me it sounded like Dimitri's relationship was coming to an end, but I was no expert and being single for an extended period only made me sound bitter if I shared this idea.

"I'm sure it will all work out," I lied, in the hopes of providing some sort of reassurance.

"Oh, remember that bar guy we met a while back?"

I searched my brain; we'd been to a lot of bars in the last few months. Trying to recall one random stranger was not an easy task.

"You'll have to give me a refresher."

"He was the waiter at the sports bar we had drinks at a while back, the one right off the N train."

"Oh yeah, the sort of Asian looking white guy, right?"

"Yeah."

"Whatever happened to him? The last I remember he was following you home from the bar."

Weeks, maybe even months earlier, Dimitri, Larry and I hit this sports bar near their apartments in Astoria that had an amazing happy hour. The waiter/bartender was a perfectly pleasant gay that kept circling back to chat with us. He was visibly interested in Dimitri; unfortunately it was Larry that had an interest in our stout waiter.

Exchanging numbers as we left, we invited our new friend to join us after his shift at Elixir, a gay bar not too far from the restaurant. Much to my surprise he did show up several hours later. By then I was beyond intoxicated, ranting and slurring my words to the point I accidentally shattered a full beer all over a drag queen sitting next to me. It turned out she was in a good mood, rather than ripping my head off she comforted me, which was necessary as I was noticeably disturbed over the loss of beer.

The Bar Guy, from what I recall, was all over Dimitri. On the walk home we took the long route to try and wear off some of the booze and hopefully get him in a cab or on a bus home. This failed as we arrived at the train before figuring out where he lived. Like a good friend, I ditched Dimitri to sit on the sticky subway floor and wait for my train.

"That night I walked him home, he was trashed."

"That makes two of us."

"You didn't go in for dessert?" I probed jokingly, knowing the guy wasn't Dimitri's type. He liked muscular gingers, two things this guy was not.

"Hardly. It wasn't easy getting away but I did. We've stayed in touch, he's a nice guy."

"That's cool."

"Actually, it's been kind of weird," Dimitri explained. "He sent me a text early the other morning, saying he needed someone to talk to."

Messages like this generally mean one of two things, you are about to be dumped or someone is about to reveal some awful truth.

"What about?"

"I met him for coffee and he told me he was raped."

"Raped?"

"Yeah."

"Wait, can a guy be raped?" I asked, most men were promiscuous, making it seem almost impossible for a rape to happen outside of those between clergymen and little boys.

"He said he went on a Grindr date with some guy, they went back to his place for a drink, and the next thing he knew he was waking up in the morning without pants on."

"Wow, that's crazy. Was he drugged?"

"Maybe."

"I hope the guy used a condom."

"That's the scary part," Dimitri exclaimed, green eyes flaring.

"Scarier than boy rape?"

"Bar Guy's been feeling sick the last few days and went to the doctor because he's convinced the guy gave him HIV."

Rape or not, this was the worst thing that could happen to anyone in my mind.

"Does he?" I asked, desperate to know the outcome.

"They don't know for sure. He isn't testing positive, but they said it could be seroconversion."

"What's that?"

"Something about HIV being in the very early stage before the virus has replicated in your system enough to show up on a test. He has to wait a few months before they can test him again."

"Is he freaking out? I'd be shitting myself."

"He's definitely scared. He's afraid to talk to his usual friends which is why he reached out to me."

Gay or straight, HIV is one of those things no one wants to catch. It's a life changing moment that you can't undo. Even with all of the advances in medicine and attempts to change the stigma, people still have certain thoughts and feelings about anyone who is HIV positive. If Bar Guy was positive, his life would be completely different; from family to dating it was a ripple effect that would stick with him forever.

"Can they do anything in the meantime to help him, or try and prevent the virus from spreading if he does have it?" I asked, slightly embarrassed I wasn't better educated on the subject.

"They have him taking PrEP, which is usually taken to prevent catching the virus."

"At least it's something."

Dimitri and I continued our discussion of reckless dating and how easy it was for people to take advantage. Both being single we could easily fall into the same trap as Bar Guy, though I feel we're both too self-aware to fall prey to anything more than mental attacks.

"I need to get back to work, it's already been an hour."

"You know if you're late they'll have to lock you in the crazy ward and allow patients to have their way with you," I mocked.

"God that would be a nightmare. I was fixing a computer upstairs the other day and some guy thought I was a doctor. He kept screaming at me to let him out."

"Now my joke is less funny, that's disturbing."

"It's literally nuts."

"Nice. I should go too. I'm meeting Leo tonight."

"Second date?"

"I'm going to say no, I think it will turn out to be more sofa warming and TV watching, followed by uncomfortable sleep and a little light dog biting."

"Lucky you. Anyway, I'll see you later."

Waving as Dimitri headed for the door I packed up my laptop and prepared to leave.

"Are you done with this table?"

Looking up from my bag, a Latin guy in a stripped tank top and black shorts stood with an iced coffee and bagel.

"Yeah, it's all yours."

"Thanks, I'm West," he said, stretching out a hand as he tried to balance bagel and coffee in the other.

As our hands connected and shook, the bagel released, projecting forward and onto the leg of my pants.

"*Oh my god*, I'm so sorry, let me grab a napkin."

"It's ok, usually I don't cream my pants for a guy that fast."

"What? Oh, that's funny," said West, handing me a handful of brown napkins.

Scooping the cream cheese from my thigh and tossing the creamy napkins into the wastebasket, I recomposed myself.

"Let me make a better first impression. I'm West, would you like to grab a drink sometime?"

West was definitely my type. Latin guy: Dark hair and eyes, not dressed over the top and apparently nice to the point of clumsy.

"Sure, a drink can't hurt. Though I can't promise you'll make a mess of my pants again," I smiled, taking out a pen. "Let me see your cup."

West held out the cup, I wrote my number up the sleeve intended for hot drinks.

"Don't lose that," I said, leaving West with the table and my number.

10. Limbo

When someone blows you off, it's best to make other plans rather than sit in your apartment stewing. That's exactly what I did as Leo informed me he was meeting friends for dinner and didn't know when, or if, he'd be free later. Angry was an understatement; he didn't need to wait until the last minute to cancel - such a dick move.

As it would happen, Dimitri and Larry were having drinks in Astoria. Though a train ride to Queens wasn't my first choice, it was a far better option than being home alone and pissed, that would almost certainly lead to text messages I'd regret later.

Getting to Astoria takes two trains which translate to one express stop and four local stops. A physical distance of only a mile or two, and a minimum travel time of forty minutes when you factor in walking to and from the train as well as waiting for both trains, which run on their own time and almost always pull away right as you enter the station.

The generally bitter train gods were shinning down on me a 5 train was pulling into the station as I came to the bottom of the stairs. Being the middle of summer, the subway station was a type of hot that felt like the air could support your full weight if you were to lean forward. Not to mention there was a ripe stench of urine from the friendly homeless neighbors that used the stairwells to do their business. The train pulled in forcing the air to move, a moment of cool as it rushed forward, followed by beads of sweat that reminded you it was hotter than the seventh circle of hell.

Inside the train car wasn't any better. The air conditioner of the car I boarded was functioning, this I know as the breeze whisked over the top of my head, but the number of bodies crammed inside the small car sucked up every bit of cool. Sweating was unavoidable, but I didn't like people to see me doing so outside the gym. In an effort to keep sweat from forming on my forehead I wiped at it in a motion intended to appear as if I was fixing my hair by pulling it to the side. In reality, it probably looked like I was fighting invisible demons away from my eyes. Even that was useless as the sides of my tank top were beginning to show the signs of an overheated body. My god, how long was it going to take to get to 59th Street?

Transferring to the N train didn't improve the situation. People shoving into the undersized stairwell, designed for a distant past, climbing two flights to reach the dual platform that had trains rushing to Queens on one side and Downtown on the other. Strangers banging shoulders and pushing forward to rush the train cars, the Queens-bound train twice as crowded as the last train. Escaping at Broadway I was able to regain my breath and personal space after a ride comparable to being inside a human sardine can.

I'd been considering a move to Queens, the apartments were bigger, newer and less expensive. But getting my mind to accept leaving Manhattan again was causing more internal angst than was worth the effort. An amazing new high-rise opened just a few blocks from Dimitri's and was close enough to the train that it wasn't a terrible walk. When I scheduled a viewing the agent no-showed which put me off the building and gave me a reason to not make the change...sometimes the smallest thing can help with justifying enormous rents for miniature spaces.

"You made it," Dimitri greeted me, pulling open the door, my only friend living in and owning an actual house.

"You don't have to hug me, I'm all sticky and sweaty from the walk."

"Larry said the same thing when he got here."

"It's a thousand degrees. I'm not even sure all the sweat is mine after the train ride."

"Well, we have wine to make you feel better."

Friends and wine, best combination for a hot day...and any day in general. A benefit to owning a house, Dimitri had a yard and was able to host barbecues. I'm always picky about what I eat, especially red meats, but after a few bottles of wine I'll stick just about anything in my mouth. By looking at the mounds of food you could assume others were coming, but the three of us devoured the homemade burgers and fries, erasing a day or two worth of gym time.

"What's going on with that French guy you were seeing?" I asked Larry, pouring myself another generous glass of delicious red wine.

"I don't know. We've had a few more dates; I'm just not feeling it. I've also been seeing another guy, Mark, who lives in Jersey."

"Eek, long distance dating."

"It's not so bad, just a quick bus ride from the Port Authority. But Mark likes to smoke weed all day, which gets old fast."

"What does he do for work?" I asked, curious as to how a stoner survived in our modern age of long work hours and limited personal time.

"He's not working right now, he's collecting unemployment."

"Good to see our tax dollars hard at work."

"Seriously, right? It's like get off your ass and do something. I'm fine if he wants to smoke once in a while, but every day is overkill. Which is why I don't know if I want to date him."

"I don't think it matters, if you move on to the next guy he'll be screwed up in some other way." My opinion file was blowing open as the wine continued to pour.

"What about the guy you've been dating, how's that going?" Larry asked, unaware I had planned on seeing Leo but ended up in Queens instead.

"It's bullshit."

"I thought he was a nice guy?"

"His personality is nice, he's not rude or anything, but I think we're playing a game that I don't know the rules to. Like tonight, he cancelled last minute to hang out with his friends. I'm fine if he wants to see them, but don't wait until you're supposed to meet up with me to say, 'never-mind.'"

"What'd you say when he cancelled?" Larry asked, Dimitri topping off both our glasses.

"Nothing. I just let it go and made plans to come play here."

"You should let him know it bothers you."

"Right now I'm trying to resist the urge to drunk text him and say something stupid that I'll be mortified by later. Plus, I can't tell him it bothers me, then he'll know I like him."

"But you do like him."

"And that's why he can't know."

"Are you sure you're not playing a game?"

"I'm almost surely positive." Did that only make drunk-sense?

"I think he just wants to be fuck buddies," Dimitri added, joining us at the table.

I considered the option taking in the backyard for the first time. This was my first barbecue attendance; the yard was larger than anything I'd seen in the city. The wooden fence, tall enough to block the neighbors on both sides, the umbrella over the table offering some shade to make the heat tolerable. A small patch of grass with a tree just beyond the table would be perfect to spread out on after another glass of wine.

"I'm not good at casual sex. I mean, I am if it's a one-time thing, but if I see a guy more than once and we keep fooling around my brain kicks into dating mode, even if I don't want it to."

"So, stop seeing him," Dimitri added, taking a drag from his cigarette, which looked appealing in this hazy moment.

"That's too logical. You know I like to make things as difficult as possible...it gives me something to write about. Let's talk about something else."

Discussing Leo was making me want to grab the phone from my pocket and start sending messages. Hopefully, if we drank enough the idea would be erased.

"How'd your book signing go?" Larry asked, kindly taking the conversation in a different direction.

Larry was my height, dark hair, hazel eyes and a quick sense of humor that meant we had to be friends. He and Dimitri were both New York natives, giving me a new perspective on the city, many of my friends being transplants like myself. Though we had bonded through humor, music was a major factor in cementing our friendship, me loving music before my time and these two knowing everything there is to know about all and any music of the 80's.

"The signing was sort of a joke, I know I'm not famous so there's no choice but to do whatever the publisher wants, but it would be nice if one of my books could garner enough attention to free me from, *New Author Nights.*"

"Did you at least sell out of books?"

"Almost, actually there was a silver lining to that event."

"What?" Dimitri asked, putting on Duran Duran.

"There was this pilot guy at the signing and we went for drinks after."

"You hooked up with a stranger in Jersey?" Dimitri asked, a note of disgust in his voice.

"You say that like I should feel some shame, which I probably would, except for, *holy giant penis.*"

"How big was it?" Larry asked, a question any respectable gay had to ask.

"It's the closest I've come to having sex with a black guy. Actually, it was so big I think he gets to be an honorary black guy."

"That sounds terrifying."

"I couldn't sit properly for a week."

"Giant dicks are a waste, most guys don't know what to do with it if it's that big," Dimitri added.

"You only say that because you're a top. You probably get big dicked lazy bottoms that just want to lay there and take it."

I had to cheers Larry for that one. It's true that a big penis didn't guarantee a good time, but it didn't hurt to see at least one giant penis now and then.

"Are you going to see his big dick again?" Larry asked, opening a new bottle of wine.

"Probably not. I took his number, but he's not in the city and I don't travel for penis."

"Maybe you should sleep with him again to distract you from Leo."

"Then I'd just fixate on the other guy. Apparently, I'm nuts."

After debating my sanity and demolishing two more bottles of wine, the Sun began to set and it was time to drag my drunken ass back to the train. Larry walked with me, almost equally drunk. His house was on the way to the train, so it gave me one last chance to vent.

"I jusss don't underssstand him," I could hear the drunk words dragging, my brain and lips unable to coordinate.

"Maybe he's just one of those guys that likes to keep it light, nothing too serious."

"But he told me he'sss not ssssleeping with any other people. Why would he tell me that if it'sss jussst sex?"

"That's kind of weird. Are you guys being safe?" Larry asked, curious if our casual sex had gone condom free.

"Not entirely," I admitted.

"I'd suggest wrapping it up as long as it's in casual limbo."

"I know, it'sss ssstupid of me."

"We all do it at some point. This is my street. Be safe."

We hugged, Larry turning left as I continued on the last block to the train. The station was elevated, meaning there were many steps to climb, an exhausting task in my current state. Once on the platform I gave into the weight of my body, sitting on the ground against one of the green pillars that held up a small roof to protect straphangers from the elements.

My phone began to vibrate, fidgeting to get it out of the pocket prison, there was a new message from Leo: *What are you up to?* Now you text me? *Heading home from Queens.* If he is booty calling me, it will be beyond annoying. *Want to come over?* Would it be totally inappropriate to scream here on the platform? *And do what?* I was fairly confident Leo was looking to get laid, but I was too buzzed to make it simple. *Just hang and watch a movie.*

If Leo had asked me to come over and watch a movie three hours earlier I probably would have jumped at the chance. Sitting drunk, on a sticky slab of concrete didn't exactly encourage me to make the effort and head over. Plus, I was still annoyed he ditched me earlier. *Sitting on your couch and watching TV isn't exactly a thrilling night.* I sent the message and instantly wished I could recall it like a bad email. Now, not only would Leo know I'm high strung, he'd probably think I'm an asshole. *Ok, didn't realize you hated it so much.*

Of course he responded, why couldn't he just ignore the message like he usually did? *I'm just saying, I want to go out and do something now and then. Unless you just want to have sex, is that your goal?* Now my fingers had a mind of their own and the words were flowing. The train was approaching and the annoying icon wasn't popping up on my screen to tell me the person on the other end was crafting a response.

Shit, the train was here and no response. It was possible that my casual sex was at an end. Maybe I should give Paul the Pilot a call and shift obsession onto someone that replies.

11. Confessional

"I despise both of you for being in relationships," I declared, this was the first time in weeks I'd seen the Animator and Business in person.

"You only say that because you're single," said Business, defending both of them.

"That's not true," my retort snippy. "I properly neglected my last relationship to the point that it withered and died on top of a twink."

"You're such a good boyfriend," added the Animator.

"I'm going to ignore the sarcasm and take the compliment."

Brunch wasn't my favorite of activities, but getting my friends around a table was, and this brunch was long overdue.

"Just thirty-seven more days," said Business.

"Until what?" I asked, perplexed by the random declaration.

"Your birthday."

"I thought you'd finally stopped counting."

"Nope."

"What's the plan for your birthday?" asked the Animator, more interested in the mimosa that had just run dry.

"Same as every year. Drink until I feel twenty, climb on something and dance, climb on someone and screw and then follow it up by passing out on my bathroom floor. Which I am completely prepared for this year as I have a brand new rug that is extra soft."

"You have the best priorities."

"We need to do something special, you're turning thirty," Business insisted, under the assumption that thirty was extremely important.

"I don't have time to plan anything more than a night of binge drinking. I'm drowning in deadlines from my editor who wants a new book and professors who want papers."

"Why'd you take classes over the summer?" asked the Animator, his face showing shock over my decision to continue the pursuit of unnecessary education.

"I don't know. I just need to do something. I feel listless."

"That's stupid," the Animator kindly tacked on to my remark.

"It's true though. You both have boyfriends; Lacee is popping out babies and has a boyfriend. Somehow I ended up on the island of misfit singles and you two never come to visit."

"But you like being single," said a confused Business.

"I like it, but it's annoying watching everyone else move ahead in their lives while I sit here writing about what's supposed to happen."

"Make something happen," said the Animator. "Go hunt down the pilot guy or the Leo person and have some fun."

"Ok, Paul the Pilot was nice, but I'm pretty sure that was a one-time thing. And Leo, he makes me crazy...the bad kind of crazy."

"You'll always be crazy. You're a writer, it's part of the persona."

"Thank you for the vote of confidence," I grumbled, giving the Animator a death glare.

"Well, I hate to eat and run, but I need to run by Duane Reade and then Drew's place."

"Of course you do." A sudden bout of relationship intolerance had taken hold.

"How is Drew?" asked the Animator.

This was the first time he'd taken interest in another person's dating life. Who was he and where was my cynical friend?

"We're good. Drew has face AIDS so he can't leave his apartment."

"What's face AIDS? Is that like herpes?" I asked, it wasn't every day you heard someone had *face AIDS*.

"No, it's just a bad infection that broke his face out in this nasty rash. Here, look." Business pulled up a photo of his boyfriend, flashing his phone at our side of the table.

It looked like a mug shot after someone had taken a hammer to the face. Drew's one eye was swollen with a massive purple lump below, his lips double their normal size and a rash covering his chin.

"What the hell is that?" asked the Animator, his face showing enough repulsion for the both of us.

"I can't remember the exact name of what it is, but usually kids get it because of their weak immune systems."

"Do you have it, and is it contagious?" My inner germaphobe was coming out to play.

"It is contagious, but I don't have it and you can only get it if you're sick and around the person."

"I'm literally going to run home and take a fistful of vitamins." This was the scariest thing I'd seen all day, including the man shitting in the subway car on my ride over.

"I'll see you guys later. No touching just in case I might infect you," Business joked as he grabbed his bag and headed for the drugstore.

"I should go too, Gary is waiting for me."

"You could have brought him."

"I know, I'm just not ready for him to hang out with all of us."

"As I said, I despise your relationship."

"You'll eventually learn to just hate it like an itch you can't scratch. See you later."

I waved the Animator off, left alone at the singles table. Meaning I was also left alone to my thoughts, which at this moment were more taunting than usual. Perhaps just hungry for attention, I pulled the phone from my pocket to search my old text messages.

Two weeks earlier, West, the random coffee encounter had sent a message to which I withheld a reply. Bingo, there was his request to meet, now would he reply to my delayed acceptance.

"It's nice to see you," said West, rising from his seat to hug me.

"You too." I sat, placing my coffee on the table.

"You brought your own coffee to a coffee date at a coffee shop?"

"I did."

"Can I ask why?"

"If I answer it's going to sound creepy."

"I think we already crossed that line when you arrived with the coffee," West grinned.

"Alright, since this is a local coffee place, I have no idea how they'll make my latte. On the flip side, if I bring my corporate coffee with me, I can focus on you and not the scary hipster barista's work."

"Fair enough. That doesn't sound creepy. Eccentric, but not creepy."

"That's a kind evaluation."

"So, can I ask you something?"

"If it's about the coffee, I just really love my Starbucks."

"No," West laughed. "How come it took you so long to reach out?"

"Good question."

It was inevitable that I was going to have to answer this, which I knew the moment I sent the request to meet. But it didn't make the answer any easier. Admit my mental gymnastics type fears of people, particularly nice people that I don't understand. Or, lie and blame it on AT&T and my iPhone's ability to hide text messages so deep within itself that they are at times undiscoverable.

"I'm sort of selfish." Hello word vomit.

West's face didn't react, I couldn't tell if my admission was intriguing or terrifying to him.

"You seemed like a really nice guy from the ten seconds of interaction when we first met. Usually if I meet a nice guy we have a date or two and then I panic."

"Are you afraid of commitment?"

"That, or maybe I'm just scared of people...or myself."

"I'll make you a deal. If you pretend I didn't throw a bagel at you, then I'll pretend you didn't hold out on meeting me for so long. Deal?" West stretched a hand over the table.

"Deal," I replied, shaking his hand, a wave of relief in his understanding.

Coffee turned into a movie. A movie turned into a glass of wine at West's apartment. Wine turned into a movie on Netflix. Not exactly the first date I had in mind, but things were flowing smoothly.

West had two businesses, one flipping real estate in Pennsylvania and another creating high end scarves for Barney's. It was crazy to think he was only a few months older than me. His apartment alone made me feel as though we were economically light-years apart. A Midtown high rise wasn't my dream apartment, but I'd be remiss to say I wasn't envious.

"What's so funny?" West asked as I unlocked our lips.
"Your mustache, it tickles."

He grinned, leaning in to continue the make-out session that reminded me of high school. In the back of my head was an image of Leo, when we kissed it felt effortless. West and I keep miss kissing, our styles not quite connecting. Pulling back again.

"Does it tickle that much?" he asked.
"I've never kissed anyone with more than stubble."
"I can trim it back if it bothers you."
"No, it's fine. I mean, if you trim it too short you'll be scratchy like me. It would probably feel like you're being re-circumcised if I go down on you right now considering I haven't shaved in a few days."
"That would be a first for me," West replied, his lips moving down my neck, his whiskers giving me goose-bumps.
"A first what?"

"I'm not cut."

Three of the most terrifying words a man can say, right up there with 'I love you' and 'I've been cheating.'

"Is that a problem?"

"Of course not...it's natural, *right?*"

"Are you sure? Because your eyes just became the size of silver dollars."

"I'm fine, maybe we should watch another movie and open another bottle of wine."

"You like Latin guys, right?"

"I do, except for the fact that you remind me that I'm as white as death."

I did like Latin guys. Leo was Latin, but he was Mexican and cut, where West was Dominican and uncut. It's like watching the same movie twice and then finding out there's extended, never-before-seen, footage or an alternate ending you didn't expect or never should have discovered.

The second movie came to an end as did the wine and it was time to either bite the bullet, which was going to come out of the pants, or make up an excuse to go home. West, who was highly affectionate in comparison to myself, gently rubbed my shoulder, giving me the eyes as I pretended not to notice by staring at the credits rolling up the flatscreen.

"I think I better get home. It's going to be a long train ride once late night service kicks in."

"You're welcome to stay."

"Thanks, but it's the first date."

It didn't matter if we were on date one or ten, when it comes to sex it's about enjoying each other. But I'd only seen two uncircumcised penises in my life. The first was on a British guy that I'd met when I first moved to the city. He stuck my hand down his pants where I discovered a semi-erect penis. A stroke that should have been short was prolonged as the skin moved over the head, revealing to my touch what was hidden inside the black trousers. I immediately made up an excuse and ran back to Jersey.

My second foreskin encounter came right before dating the Devil. I was seeing an Italian guy and trying to give foreskin a chance. It didn't look horrible on the guy, but the one time I managed to put it in my mouth the smell was like rotting flesh. Not to mention a four inch piece of white thread, probably from his underwear, wrapped around the head of his dick and dangling from my mouth by the time I realized what was happening. At that moment I swore off all foreskin.

A short kiss goodbye and I made my way through the tangled halls, down the elevator and into the street. I needed to talk to someone and get perspective on my sudden attack of fore-phobia. And there was only one person that could give me the blunt advice I needed.

"What are you doing here, it's after midnight?" asked the Animator, disregarding the fact that I had managed to get into his building without buzzing, trusting old people were so helpful when it came to doors.

"I need your advice, can I come in."

"Now isn't a good time."

"I only need a few minutes."

"Gary and I are sort of in the middle of something."

"He has foreskin," I blurted, if I couldn't enter the apartment then the words would have to enter the hallway.

"Who has foreskin?"

"West. That guy I met a few weeks back in Starbucks. The nice one."

"So."

"He has foreskin. I'm scared of foreskin. What do I do with the foreskin?"

"You have to be kidding me?"

"No, I honestly have no clue what to do."

"Are you hearing yourself?"

The Animator's head was poking through the chained door, his glasses tilted forward, eyes glaring at me with derision. Closing the door to remove the chain, the Animator came into the hallway, shutting the door behind him, but keeping a hand on the knob to prevent it from locking.

"Gary and I are trying to enjoy a little bit of time together. I don't want to be discussing foreskin with you in the middle of the night, or in my hallway for that matter."

"But *I-*"

"No, but. This is insane, you're creating drama just to create drama."

"I'm not creating drama. I *just-*"

"This is drama. Either stick the guy's dick in your mouth or don't. It's that simple. But now you need to go home because you're interrupting."

The Animator returned to the other side of the door, promptly closing it as I stood, mouth open, in his hallway trying to understand what invisible line I had crossed.

12. Turncoats

Lacee's relationship with her live-in baby daddy was verging on the definition of tumultuous. So much so, that she made the rare unannounced appearance at my apartment for midday drinks and bitching.

"I know he's fucking that Christie girl."
"That's China, right?"

Brad and Lacee had always been playing tug of war with each other's heart. They had finally reached a point where suspicions ran so high that not a day went by without a fight.

"Do you have proof?"
"I didn't catch them in the act, but he recently went on a work trip to Apple's headquarters and I found out he was allowed to take a guest."

"And you didn't want to go?" I was trying to be supportive, but this was a temper I'd never seen on Lacee, she could easily rip my head off in the heat of the moment.

"I didn't know until a few days ago. One of his work friends was at our apartment and let it slip. He also let slip that Christie went with him."

"That's pretty incriminating."

"Right? I mean, why would you take her if you're not fucking her. I mean her twat probably runs the wrong way."

I'd never seen Lacee so worked up, defensive or offensive. I liked it.

"Maybe it's like that movie, Teeth, and she's just waiting to bite the dick off of anyone that dares penetrate."

"That's gross."

"Hey, it could happen. I'm not a vagina expert, but plenty of gays tell me there's something terrifying down there."

"If you want I can bust mine out and prove them wrong."

"I'm going to take a rain check on that, for the sheer fact that I may become so transfixed that I either turn straight or twice as gay. I really can't afford either with my book deadline looming."

"Before we start talking about you and books, can we finish?"

"Yeah, sorry, just sayin'." It seemed all of my friends were in a mood lately. "Back to, how do you know if they've been sleeping together?"

"I don't think I ever told you, but a few years back, that Cece girl."

"Oh yeah, the one from Brad's birthday."

"Yeah, they had sex."

"When?"

"Right before I found out I was pregnant."

"Which time?"

"The first time."

"How'd you find out?" I asked curiously. "Also, all I have left is a little Pinot Gris, is that good?"

"Yeah, thanks." Lacee accepted the glass and continued. "After I told Brad I was pregnant he got all weepy and wanted us to both be honest about everything. He fucked her once while he was drunk a couple days before the birthday party at our apartment."

"And you were okay with that?" Staying with a cheater wasn't exactly an ideal situation.

"No, but I didn't want to break it off when we were about to have a baby."

I'd never understood the logic babies put into people's heads. If you are in an unhappy or broken relationship and you stay together for the children, often times, or at least from what I've seen, you end up damaging the children. All of the anger and resentment tends to manifest in emotional distance, rage and sometimes even physical abuse. Not that Lacee or Brad would hit their kids, but it didn't mean ten years from now their dislike of one another wouldn't spill onto their offspring like toxic runoff.

"Did you say anything to Cece?"

"About a year after I wrote her an email and told her that I didn't hold any hard feelings against her."

"But it sounds like you do." Was I missing something?

"I do and I don't. That helped me and Brad get closer, but it frustrates me that he cheated and now I'm forever paranoid he'll do it again, which is more his fault than hers."

"Did she reply to your email?" What do you say when someone forgives your sexual mistakes?

"She replied and told me it was the best thing that ever happened because she finally realized he didn't love her."

"That's a first, from the Maury show I've learned that most people assume you love them after the sex."

"She went on and on telling me how she met the *'love of her life'* and *'they're having a kid.'*"

"There's a twist for you. Though I think she's full of shit."

"What do you mean?" Lacee asked, wiggling an empty glass as an invitation for a refill.

"You don't sleep with someone's boyfriend and then become enlightened or find your happily-ever-after. I mean, the Devil screwed that guy and there's no way he then found the perfect match," I said, realizing I harbored more anger towards my ex than I wanted to be true. "I'd also never write a letter to forgive the guy."

"No, you'd just write an angry blog or nasty book about him and then avoid the pair."

"Okay, ouch."

"Sorry, but it's true. I think it was healthy to at least say something to Cece instead of just holding on to the anger."

"I didn't say it wasn't. I just said I wouldn't do that."

"It's not always about you."

"Are you on your period or something, what the hell?"

"I just need to vent about me for a minute without it becoming you and your problems."

"I'm not trying to make it about my problems. I was just offering a comparison."

"Whatever, I need to talk to one of my married friends about this."

"So, what, I'm single so my advice no longer matters?"

"No, you're just so jaded and cynical that all of your advice suggests breaking up."

"I'm the perpetual angry single person, you know that, which is why you come here when you want a nudge to break it off."

"Whatever, I have to go. Here I can't finish this." Lacee offered me the wine glass I'd just refilled.

Closing the door behind her I downed the extra glass of wine and reached out to one friend that was sure to not be on the rag.

"Maybe she's just having a bad day. It's not easy hearing someone else tell you your decisions are bad," said Business, polishing off a salad.

Still in need of advice on Leo and West and having had two friends erupt on me, Business was the one friend I could count on to remain objective or at least provide an ear.

"I guess, but what's the Animator's excuse for being so pissy?"

"He's in the dating honeymoon phase."

"Gross," I interjected."

"They were probably about to fool around when you showed up."

"But he's my go-to person for advice. If I can't count on him, who can I count on?"

"You can talk to me."

Business had good intentions and I did want to tell him my problem, but I wasn't sure foreskin was up his alley.

"C'mon, tell me," Business pushed, our entrees arriving.

I had asked him to meet me in Hell's Kitchen at VYNL. A gay establishment that had tacky chrome everywhere, decorations from the last generation's favorite music and lots of people watching, in and outside of the restaurant.

"So, West and I had a great first date, but when it came to the sex...I couldn't."

"Why, it wouldn't get hard?"

"No, everything was working as expected."

"So..."

"He has foreskin," I whispered, afraid of drawing attention to our conversation.

"Have you never seen foreskin before?"

"Of course I've seen it, I just get a little...grossed out by it. And I'm afraid if I see West's penis and it's got a ton of foreskin hanging off the end I'll be so freaked out that I won't be able to see him again."

"You know the Animator is uncut."

"I did not know that," I responded to the comment, surprised. "How do *you* know that?"

"We used to workout together and I saw it in the locker room."

"I really want to remain focused on the foreskin issue, but now I kind of want to discuss you being a locker room voyeur."

"I'm not a voyeur, I got a quick glimpse one day, no big deal. I mean, it was kind of big, but you know what I mean."

"Wow, good for the Animator on being big, but that still doesn't make me feel better about the foreskin."

"Then stop seeing him."

"But I want to see him again. Are there any tricks to make it so you can't tell it's there."

Asking the question was almost as dumb as asking if West would be willing to cut it off without a commitment.

"That I don't know. But what about the other guy you liked, why not just see where things go with him?"

"I've been trying to not talk to him."

"Why?"

"I made a fool of myself by running my mouth. I also think he's just bad for me. I mean, the sex is good, but he makes me crazy in the head."

"You are crazy in the head," said Business, having a surprising number of comments for me this evening.

"A lot of people have told me that lately. I used to think it was cute and quirky, but now you're all starting to make me think it's weird and scary."

"There's nothing wrong with being in your head all the time. I think you just spend too much time there."

I couldn't agree less with Business. My head was the safest place in the world. A place where I could hash out my mental drama without having to share everything with the people around me and paint the picture that I'm so damaged by our culture of self-narration that it may be too late to change.

"I like being in my head."

"I know, and your blogs are always really funny. They just kind of make me..." Business paused.

"They make you what?" I asked, his eyes breaking with mine, wine glass hitting his lips in an effort to end the sentence.

"What? Tell me."

"I feel a little bad for you."

"Excuse me?"

"I'm not trying to offend you."

"We might be a little bit past that point. Please tell me why you feel sorry for me." My temper was flaring. I didn't need anyone judging me, especially a friend.

"You have two nice guys that both seem to be interested and you're picking at small things to avoid dealing with either of them."

"That's not true."

"It is true."

"I don't see it that way."

"You're letting an inch of skin and something you said to someone prevent you from interacting, doesn't that seem a little absurd?"

Business had a point, but this wasn't the advice I needed or desired. The idea that I couldn't jump into a commitment wasn't new. I'd been doing the avoidance dance for so long it was now possible to consider it my character trait.

"I think you're still not over Grant."

"The Devil has nothing to do with this. This is about West and Leo. One is a dick and the other has too much dick skin."

"No, it's about you. You've told me tonight that two of your friends are complaining about your need to indulge in yourself."

"I'm not indulging, I'm trying to talk to my friends about what's going on in my life."

"I didn't mean it like that, I'm just saying maybe there's more to the situation."

"You know what, this was a bad idea."

Sitting my wine glass on the table, where the contents swirled to a stop, I put on my jacket.

"Ryan, don't go."

"It's fine. I'm going to head home and indulge in myself for a little while."

"I didn't mean it like that."

"It's fine," I snapped, pushing my chair to its home under the table. "But maybe all of you should remember that I always listen to your problems and whining and don't judge. All I asked for was the same."

I left Business at the table, heading for the train, this day needed to be over as fast as a bottle of wine and sleeping pills could make it happen.

13. Lobster

In an effort to conduct what I would consider to be research for my book, I joined OkCupid. A phone app for dating that I'd never given the time of day. Grindr was the go to app for quick and dirty hookups, which seemed like the only reason for logging on to any social app. But sex stories weren't going to provide life to an undeveloped plot. No, I needed to go on real dates. A secondary benefit would be the time spent clearing my head as my friends had gone on strike and I was still dumbfounded by West and Leo and what action to take.

After signing up and answering a few dozen personal questions I was able to browse local guys and see if we were rated as a match, friends or enemies. Of the choices I found myself most interested in those who rated high as enemies. It was like the developers were handing me a tool that said, meet this person and you'll be sure to get a good story. Thumbing through dozens of photos I looked for attractive enemies that could potentially result in an interesting plot twist or even bad boy mistake.

Enjoying myself too much, the app began sharing who I was looking at before I realized what was happening. Messages began to fill up my sad little virtual dating inbox. As I thumbed through to delete them a familiar face caught my eye. Was that Lobster? I hadn't seen him in years, but from the pasty complexion that rivaled my own, receding hairline, heavy black rimmed glasses and pouty mouth it had to be him.

When I first moved to New York, technically New Jersey, Journal Square to be specific, and lied to people about where I was living, I met Lobster on the train. I noticed him several times over a period of a few weeks. He always seemed to be in my train car, looking my way while I did my best to keep my eyes focused on anything else. My efforts to avoid his gaze resulted in finishing six books on my iPhone in under a month. He was great for motivating my reading efforts.

When Lobster, finally spoke to me he was holding a bag with a print of a lobster on the front, which I remembered vividly while not being able to retain his real name. I was so engrossed in what I was reading that I didn't notice his approach, otherwise I'd have made a quick move to the other end of the train and hopped off at the next stop, even if it meant waiting on the platform for another train. But he cornered me and my mind didn't think up an excuse quick enough, so I provided my number. Giving him a fake seemed like a bad choice considering we were on the same train with unpleasant frequency.

Lobster began sending text messages regularly, to which I replied. Admitting I enjoyed the attention gets me some credit, credit I immediately lost when Lobster finally asked me out on a date and I declined citing an imaginary boyfriend. He stopped reaching out to me for a year, then randomly texting me and starting the cycle all over. After the second go-around he finally got the message and we hadn't spoken since.

Now it was my turn to reach out. Much to my surprise, 'hello,' wasn't greeted with the appropriate, 'go fuck yourself.' Lobster seemed like a decent guy, so much so that he agreed to grab a drink at Canyon Road. It just so happened that he also lived on the Upper East Side these days. It was probably more appropriate for him to live in this neighborhood considering it's his Jewish birthright.

Canyon Road is a restaurant that I'd walked by several times but had never entered. Trying to capture an Old West theme it was beyond tacky with fake bull skulls on the wall, cowboy hats and twisted rope. It was possible to be one hundred percent certain that no one I knew would run into Lobster and I on our pseudo-date. I'd looked through all of the photos in his online profile and time hadn't been kind to his waistline.

Arriving at the restaurant the hostess, in her turquoise boots and fringe mini-skirt, sat me at the end of the bar. One classic margarita and I was feeling great. So great, that if Lobster didn't get here before I had another I'd likely end up texting one of the guys I was trying to avoid.

"Hey, you."

A hand firmly gripped my shoulder, my lips tightly holding a tiny straw as I sucked the last drops of flavor from the ice cubes in my undersized cup.

"Hey, how are you?" I stood to provide a proper hug greeting.

His pictures literally an enormous lie, he was even more round in person. My hands could barely connect with one another on the other side of him. More drinks would be in order to survive this date.

"Can I get what he's having?" Lobster spoke to the approaching bartender.

"Can I get another, please?" These were delicious margaritas, a good thing considering they were horrifically overpriced.

"It's good to see you, Robert."

"Ryan."

"I thought your name was Robert."

"It's both. I prefer to go by my last name. Robert is so formal. Plus it's my dad's name. Though he actually goes by Red because he has bright red hair down to his butt." Maybe these drinks are too strong.

"Ok, it's nice to see you, Ryan."

"You too."

"Is it?"

"Of course. I was surprised you popped up on OkCupid."

"I was surprised you sent me a message. You ignored me in Jersey, I figured you were teasing me back then, or being a bitch."

"Can we call it a bit of both?" I smiled, surprised the lobster bag man had a sense of humor.

We floated through the conversation, discovering Lobster was a lawyer. This was of no surprise. I stereotype Jews as being lawyers, accountants and other careers that involved making and managing money. At the same time I'm envious of the Jewish ability to make money, something I had never learned in my Christian upbringing. Though I was really good at spending money and putting myself in financially uncomfortable situations.

"What are you doing these days? Last time we talked you were trying to write a book."

"And I'm still trying," I smirked, stirring my dwindling drink. "I have two books out there in the world, trying to make a third happen."

"Wow, so you're actually a published author."

"Yes, I'm living the dream of impoverished authorship." Did that phrase make sense? I hope so, I was becoming too drunk to tell.

"So what's the plan?"

"What do you mean?" I asked, Lobster changing topics too quickly for me to follow.

"I mean, do you want to go back to my place, your place?"

Turns out OkCupid isn't any different from Grindr. That or I was giving off a vibe that I was looking to get laid.

"Neither," I said, Lobster giving me a blank glare.

"Then why are we here?"

"I thought it would be fun to catch up and see where things went."

"We're not friends, we don't have anything to catch up on."

For a guy of his size, Lobster was oddly confident I was going to suck his dick. Possibly the sign of an enormous penis, or some intense sexual skill that has been praised by others. The one thing I could count on, if we slept together, he would be cut. One thing the Jews got right was circumcising everyone and anything that looked like a penis.

"I'm out of here."

"*Wait-*" Lobster was out the door before I could stop him. "You didn't pay for your drinks."

"Would you like the check?" asked the bartender, having telepathy or excellent timing.

"No, but I'll take it."

With a swipe of my card the seventy-dollar, four drink, tab was paid for and I made my way home. Grateful there were only a few blocks to walk, the tequila sending my head on a trip that required soft pillows and fuzzy blankets to cure.

The next day, Dimitri invited me out for coffee on his lunch break, providing an opportunity to once more try and gain some insight into why all of my friends were upset with me. It was also a chance to share the drink fiasco from last night.

"Where've you been the last week? It's like you vanished."

"My sister had surgery so I was at my parent's house on Long Island."

"What kind of surgery?"

"They found a lump a month back and the biopsy came back as breast cancer."

"Is she ok?"

"Things look good. It was intense, she had a double mastectomy and reconstructive surgery at the same time."

"I didn't realize it could happen all at once."

"She used to work for a plastic surgeon, he advised doing it all at once. I think he just likes to recommend getting bigger tits."

"If they don't kill you, make them bigger. I think that's the slogan for breast cancer groups everywhere."

"Nice. Things are good though. Actually, while I was there I ran into a friend from high school that I haven't seen in a decade."

"How was that, awkward?" I asked, the delicious iced coffee hitting my lips as I paused to sip at the straw.

"It was weird. He's exactly the same, which is why we stopped hanging out; he's clingy and talks nonstop. I also don't think he knows I'm gay, he kept bringing up sports."

"You don't look like the average gay, you're kind of butch. I could see someone not knowing. You'd actually be the ideal closet case."

"Right? I could get away with it until a cute ginger came along."

"Be careful, you know a ginger can suck out your soul."

"That's not all they're good at sucking out."

"Gross. Hilarious. But gross."

"What's going on in your world?"

"Let's see, Animator and Lacee are both mad at me. And I blew up at Business, so I probably need to apologize to him."

"Why are they mad?"

"Lacee thinks I'm too self-involved and the Animator is annoyed I showed up at his house to complain about foreskin."

"His foreskin?" Dimitri asked, dipping his teabag, brow raised.

"No, West's. Though I can see how that could be misconstrued."

"What's wrong with it?"

"Nothing, I guess. I'm just not a fan. Which makes me worry about seeing it."

"You haven't had sex yet."

With pursed lips I shook my head. No, West and I had not had sex. I was as amazed as everyone else that I'd discovered the foreskin secondhand and not through promiscuous research.

"Just close your eyes or keeps the lights off. Once it's hard you probably won't even be able to tell he has it."

"I guess, but what if it stinks?" I asked, this was my second greatest fear after actually seeing the foreskin.

"If it smells get out of there. A guy with bad hygiene is unacceptable."

"Don't they all smell?"

"No, only if they don't take care of themselves."

"Thank you, that is rational advice, which is what I expected from the Animator."

"I wouldn't worry about it, he's been blowing me off lately. I'm thinking it's the boyfriend."

Was the Animator's boyfriend the problem? Perhaps it was some sort of relationship manipulation that I'd failed to see in the shock of being shut out.

"But I'm confused. Didn't you already sleep with West?" Dimitri asked.

"You're thinking of Leo. He's foreskin free, but I'm trying to stay off his dick as he's like a drug with unpleasant side effects."

"Why, what's going on there?"

"Nothing. I've put talking to him and West on hold. In place of seeing either of them I've decided to have a bunch of OkCupid first dates."

"Why?" Dimitri's face said the idea wasn't as brilliant as I assumed.

"I figure if I go on a bunch of first dates that I'll either start to want a relationship and go after West, or become so fed up that I only want sex and head back to Leo."

"You have interesting logic."

"So far my logic is working. I had a date last night, though it might not qualify as a first."

"How so?"

"I met the guy years ago, but found him again on OkCupid. He gained a bunch of weight, but his face looked the same. I figured it would be a good way to break the dating ice as I have zero interest in sleeping with him."

"What happened?"

"We chatted for all of forty-five minutes before he asked if we were going to bang. I said no and he left."

"Sounds like a typical OkCupid date."

"That's a Grindr date, this stupid app is supposed to be different. Also, he left me with the tab. Talk about a douche."

Dimitri and I finished our conversation and drinks before he headed back to work and I headed back to my laptop. I was determined to get a good story out of OkCupid and self-help myself until I made up my mind on which guy to choose.

14. Re-penis

With a new virtual ally to guide me through the world of dating, I was setting up dates for each night of the week to build a nice catalogue of tales. If my editor wanted dirt and drama I was going to do my best to deliver.

Kareem was next on my dating agenda, inviting me to attend a series of six ten-minute plays. His friend was acting in one and he had directed another. This was also an opportunity to meet in a public place in case he was an Internet weirdo and wanted to chop me up into bite size pieces.

I was underwhelmed by Kareem's in person appearance. He was above average by normal standards, but far below New York gay standards. It's like he'd yet to be introduced to the concept of a gym. A big turnoff as I was compulsive about going daily. His short curly hair looked greasy and it was hard to tell if he was sweaty in general or just nervous. Either way the sweat marks were growing under his arms and standing out against the blue and white plaid.

Reminding myself that this wasn't a date, but research, we headed to a small theater on 47th Street that you would never know existed, at least I didn't. A dank little space where canned beer and boxed wine were served in the lobby that consisted of a wooden box with a hipster guy behind, just waiting to shed on anyone that dare approach. The stage itself wasn't terrible; fold-up chairs four rows deep on a two-tier black platform for better viewing.

The first play was something about a mother calling into a radio program for advice on her bodysuit wearing son. The lead was good, but overall it was dull and the son dancing around while thrusting his dick in the face of front row patrons was unappealing. Kareem's play was decent, the crazy relationship between New Yorkers, garden spaces and the desire to have a personal plot. The three actors pulled it off nicely.

But the last play was my favorite. It was demented. A dinner party where the guests cooked their own body parts and fed them to the other attendees. It wrapped up with one actress singing about basting her body is piss before seasoning and cutting off her arm to the audience's delight. The perfect way to wrap up sixty minutes of ass killing pain

The date came to a close quickly, Kareem being invited to the after party and me knowing a room with drinks and a sweaty guy was a bad idea. Instead, I said goodnight and met up with my friend Shew for a late happy hour at Hardware Bar around the corner. Overall, it wasn't a highly entertaining date, but who can resist staged self-mutilation?

On the next date was Johnny, or as I should probably call him, the Hands Guy. We met at a bar where he was actually a bartender. I can't tell if this counts as a date or me just meeting him at work. In my defense, he failed to share before meeting that we were going to his place of employment...while he was on duty. Come to think of it, maybe he's a genius, who doesn't want to date on corporate time?

Not at all my type, Johnny's tall, blonde and a bit pudgy, what I did like was his ability to turn a phrase and be a little bitchy. We chatted as he serviced the other patrons around the bar. Leaving in between my beer sips to ensure the masses were satisfied. It turned out he was saving to open his own bar. Rather than shit all over his dream, I nodded my head and provided kudos for his aspiration. In reality, a nearly forty-something bartender probably won't be owning an establishment any time soon. But stranger things have happened, after all someone keeps publishing my ranting's.

Johnny wasn't drinking with me, but he was accepting shots from guys farther down the bar. Who knows what the pink concoction was or how many he had, I tried not to look to ensure no one thought I was interested, but after Johnny became friendlier it was extremely difficult. First grabbing my hands over the bar and rubbing them. He told me how smooth they were. I of course made a masturbation joke and blamed it on years of lotion abuse.

Hand rubbing progressed as he returned from a trip to the restroom and tried to stick a finger down the back of my pants. Unsure of what he was trying to do I smacked away the probing finger, convinced that he was pulling the straight-guy-vagina-finger-smell trick. That was enough to send me packing. If you want your fingers to smell like ass it's probably better to find a cheap hooker, I wasn't about to become anyone's finger bate.

Then there was Allen, who looked like he might be a white-Asian mix of some sort. Rather than I ask it was easier to assume and decide for myself. Especially when asking could bring up family and a deep discussion I couldn't care less to hear about.

This one did have a bit of a wild side, asking me out for coffee, which turned into a drink, which turned into a visit to the Ritz. The crowd was wild for a Thursday night the summer heat encouraging everyone to go either shirtless or in the sluttiest tank tops to be mass-produced. Allen was quick to hit the bar and bring back drinks, citing his ability to drink without end. I was compelled to test the idea, I felt my Irish liver gave me the advantage, but I also made the wise choice to stick with beer and not break into mixed beverages. Allen was living dangerously and mixing any and everything.

Upstairs the bar had a special treat, the small dance floor had a stripper pole, plopped on a box right in the middle. Gays and the hags that love them took turns climbing on and doing their best whore impressions. Clothes came off, a few girls tumbled off their dramatically tall heels and one guy tried to crowd surf, without success, off of the box.

I'm guessing to woo me, Allen decided he would give the pole a go. He climbed up, slid down, swung around and was surprisingly acrobatic. The crowd cheered, even I was impressed, he was clearly well versed in riding large poles. And as gloriously as it had begun it ended, the pull ripped out of the ceiling, plummeting backwards and sending Allen into the crowd. The pole coming to a rest as it shattered the mirror that covered the back wall, gays scattering to get away from the shards that were raining down. Allen was flat on his back, the DJ coming over to help him up.

I took my cue to sit my drink on the floor and slip out of the club. There was no way I was getting fingered as the boyfriend of the guy that just tore up the dance floor. That could be expensive.

Who doesn't want to date a doctor? I thought everyone until I went out with Dr. Rick the prick. He invited me for coffee at his 'favorite spot,' Java Girl. It was exactly eighteen blocks down from my apartment. Farther than I wanted to walk for a date, but the weather was good so there was no excuse to cancel.

There was some surprise as I arrived and an angry little gay man was standing outside of a closed Java Girl. Dr. Rick didn't know his favorite coffee place was closed on Tuesdays. While he recommended a teashop on the next avenue I nodded and did a visual inspection. He was fit, but his hair was receding from the front and patching in the back. If I stood too close it was likely that I'd walk away with short strands of black on my sleeve. Wait, make that my pant leg. There's at least six inches in height difference between us, I'm never the tall one.

At the teashop I was forced to admit I hate tea, but as luck and corporate planning would have it, a Starbucks was directly next door. My suggestion was that I go grab a real coffee and come back over. Either Dr. Rick was truly annoyed or thought I would run off and not return. Declining my offer he surrendered to my addiction and accompanied me to Starbucks where he ordered a sugar loaded drink, odd for a doctor.

Droning on and on about his work and saving lives each day I counted the number of people that walked by wearing headphones, sixty-seven. Then the number of dogs that went past the window, seventeen, four of which were Pugs. He caught my attention when mentioning he was moving to Atlanta at the end of the month.

Moving? If you're moving what the hell are we doing on a date together? Not only is it a waste of my time, but I should have let you pay for my coffee when you offered because I will certainly never see you again. That was enough for me. I lied and said I had to get back to work. It was after six but he had failed to ask what I do for work. For all Dr. Rick knows I could work a night shift flipping burgers...or prostituting. Both require great skill when it comes to handling meat.

One dating disaster worth recounting came before I pissed the Animator off. We've all encountered at least one crazy drunk person at a bar that won't leave us alone. This isn't a date, but it may as well have been because I could have sealed the deal if only I was willing to pull my pants down around the corner.

The Animator forced his new boyfriend Gary to be social and meet up for a drink at Duplex when they first began dating. It was early on a Saturday and there was sure to be no one around, the best time of day to drink. Managing to arrive on time even after extensive train delays, we ordered a round and sat at the back of the bar to chat.

All was going well until a man came to stand between the Animator and myself. He started speaking as if he knew one of us, me assuming he knew the Animator and him assuming the reverse. The man chattering, ordering a drink and then pulling up a stool to the side of me. While caressing my arm it became clear that drunk was not a strong enough term for whatever was going on with this guy.

I have no issue with older guys, but if you're going to hit on me and be fifty at least be semi sober, or make sure I'm completely shit faced. His drink was slow to come, giving him time to tell me how he loved gingers. My hair is dirty blonde and nothing irritates me more than being called ginger. Yes, my facial hair gets a little red, but I make sure to shave it off daily so no one knows the truth. If only that was the worst of his comments.

Never sharing his name, the man did share that he lived around the corner. He also shared that he would love to take me home and fuck me. This was obviously a huge compliment to me. He seemed surprised when I declined, actually asking for a reason why I refused to be fucked by a stranger. Now was the moment the bartender decided to bring his beer. He then ordered me a beer, which I immediately declined. You take their drinks and you take their dicks.

The best part of all this was when he became annoyed at my refusal, tossing his card at the bartender to cash out and then discovering his card was declined. He quickly returned to being a sweet, drunk stranger, inviting me to cover his drink. I was prepared to argue, but the bartender jumped right in and took control, forcing drunky to find the eight dollars for his beer.

These dating mishaps have an interesting effect on me. I don't feel vindicated in having been around the block without needing to pull my pants down. It was the opposite, I feel like there is no hope out there and the number of assholes so greatly outnumbers the nice guys that there is only one way to rectify things: Sleep with Leo.

A normal person would have taken this opportunity to run to West. I wasn't taking him off of the dating playing field, but after the butt fingers, piss plays and drunken wanna-rape there was only one thing that had any appeal: Sex. Leo was definitely in the top ten of what I'd had over the years, which according to Business is, 'a lot.'

I spent the next week commuting to and from Leo's in the evening to hump and then be bitten by his dog as I made quick escapes to head home and shame shower. I wasn't any closer to figuring out who I wanted, or if I wanted anyone, but at least I was getting a reward for all of the effort.

15. Brakes

An evening of alcohol-fueled excitement resulted in falling asleep on Dimitri's couch in a rather uncomfortable position. The deep grey-blue cushions made it possible to lay back while having your head upright. This position was doom on your neck after a few hours. I hadn't intended on spending the night, especially when I had a meeting with my editor bright and early the following morning.

The unexpected onslaught of sleep meant no alarm set and no time to get ready. Equivalent to a work walk of shame. Leaving from Queens also wasn't in my plan for the morning. When I woke there was just over forty minutes to get myself into the city. Not taking any chances I called for a car, splashing water on my face, trying to smooth my cockeyed hair and stretch the wrinkles out of my shirt.

Rush hour exists on trains, but it means you push harder and get inside before the doors threaten to close on you like your life hangs in the balance. Rush hour in a car is a totally different thing. The car arrived and the driver was all too polite, telling me some nonsense about sports scores while I panicked from the backseat. *We weren't going to make it on time, it's impossible.*

"Don't worry, my friend. I know a shortcut." The scariest thing any cab driver can say.

Shortcut? There's no shortcut. Every road is clogged with cars, intersections at a standstill as police try to motion cars forward. Where was the mute button on the driver? Maybe he's on Bluetooth, he can't possibly be rambling to me. And the radio, how the hell do you turn it off. The volume up option works, is the down seriously broken? This is the cad from hell.

A glimpse of hope arrived as the Brooklyn Bridge came into site and the car began to creep up the curved lane that would grant access to the side of the river I needed to be on in sixteen minutes. Bailing out of the car and running the bridge was beginning to seem like a good idea. Then again, getting to a meeting covered in sweat may actually be worse than looking like a tired hooker.

After what felt like an eternity we made it over the bridge and to the final stop light between the meeting and me. Instead of patiently waiting, I handed over two twenties and exited the cab. Walking past three cars I reached the crosswalk, the light still red, a cement barrier stopped me from cutting across traffic. There was only one way across this street and it was the crosswalk.

Like dead weight, I hit the ground, skidding a few feet, my arm hot from rubbing across the blacktop. Temporarily stunned, I got to my feet, eyes searching for an explanation. A few feet away a bicyclist was picking up his overturned bike. My brain caught up to the situation at the sight of spinning wheels.

"What the fuck is wrong with you? You don't watch where you're going? It's a fucking red light you bike riding asshole!"

Without a response the bike messenger hopped on the black seat, speeding away. Raising my hand to flip him off a pain shot through my wrist. Oh shit, it was like a hot iron was being pressed through the center. Did I break it? No, it can't be broken if I'm able to move it. Shit, only three minutes to make my meeting.

Stepping out of the street, crowds watching from both sides, no one attempting to ask if I was ok after the outburst. To make matters worse, the farther I walked, the more my ankle hurt, my wrist swelling and turning an interesting shade of purple. No matter the pain, I was going to make it on time and now I had a good reason for looking a mess.

Emily and I agreed to meet at the City Hall Starbucks. It was convenient when I was coming from home, the 6 train let out half a block away and Emily could easily get here from Brooklyn. Entering, the coffee house was packed, people at every table, a long line wrapping from the register, around the pastry case and right to the door where new patrons were deciding against coffee and continuing on their way to work. Emily didn't appear to be here; maybe I could clean myself up in the restroom quickly.

"Mr. Ryan." A stranger in a grey pinstripe suit approached with an outstretched palm.

"Do I know you?"

"I'm John Wright, Senior Editor of non-fiction for Play House Books."

"It's nice to meet you. I thought Emily was going to be here," I said, confused why a random editor had appeared.

"Yes, that's what I'm here to discuss."

"Okay, let me just grab a coffee-"

"I have a skinny vanilla latte at my table for you."

"Oh, thanks." I followed John to his table near the Broadway facing window. "How did you know my drink?"

"I like to know everything about my authors."

"Your authors?" Now I was truly lost.

"But first, are you ok? I can't help but notice you're holding your arm in an unusual way and you have blood on your forehead and shoulder."

Glancing at my shoulder, John was right, an asphalt stained tear in my shirt revealed a bloody scrape. Through touch I could feel the drying blood above my temple.

"I'm fine, just a minor incident on my way here involving a bike."

"Would you like to reschedule?"

My wrist and hand were throbbing, moving my fingers caused little pangs to shoot up the length of my arm. Rescheduling was the wise decision.

"It's really ok. Where's Emily?"

"I hate to share this, but Emily is no longer with our publishing house."

"What, why?" Did she take another job? Selfish bitch.

"You may not be aware but you are the only author on Ms. Jensen's roster."

"Seriously?"

"Yes, and for that reason we have decided to consolidate her authors, you, to my roster."

"What does that mean for my contract?"

"To be honest your last book performed mediocre at best. Play House will honor your current contract for one additional book. However, if the publication doesn't result in the sell of at least twenty-five thousand copies we will not be requesting additional works."

Twenty-five thousand copies, this guy must have smoked crack on his way here. My first book barely hit those numbers and the last one hadn't reached the ten thousand mark. It's like I was being broken up with in the politest way possible, or given a mercy fuck before the dump.

"Does this impact the content Emily requested I focus on?"

"Not necessarily. Emily was focused on selling sex. Not a terrible tactic, but your audience is small in comparison to others. For example the tween category has seven times the readership of your homosexual base."

"Are you saying I can continue writing the current book or produce something you can sell to everyone?"

"It's only a suggestion. Personally, your novel amuses me, the writing is there, but the consumers are not. On that note, I need to be getting to the office for another meeting. Here's my card, feel free to reach out if you have questions."

My new least favorite editor placed a card on the circular table and exited the building. I wasn't going to let his polite bullying change my book. If it didn't sell, it didn't sell. Making something I enjoy was more important even if that meant I would be back on the publisher hunt, my new greatest fear.

Ignoring the pain in my hand was not proving victorious. Finally surrendering I made my way to Bellevue Hospital. Stupid imitation subway signs greeted me as I tried to figure out where to go, it had been years since I'd walked into a hospital. Who here can help me?

The information line was at least thirty people deep; screw waiting in line. Walking through a long, pale brick corridor I found the ER. Every chair full, but a nurse behind Plexiglas was free.

"Hi," I said, trying to get her attention.

"Fill out the clipboard, bring it back and wait to be called."

"Okay." Taking the clipboard I clumsily filled out the many, many questions as best possible with my gimp arm and no place to sit.

As it turned out, completing the intake form was the easiest part of my hospital visit. When my name was called the triage nurse took me into a room so small it was impossible to move without the two of us touching. She noted my height, weight, issue and sent me back to find a hard, cold plastic waiting chair. It was small consolation knowing the rounded green chair now available had been waiting in this place since the late seventies from the look of things.

"Robert Ryan," called a heavy female voice.
"Here, right here." I was elated to finally be called.

The wait stretched into seven hours all leading to this moment. My non-critical issue allowed several homeless people on the hunt for painkillers to go ahead, one girl with a leg that bent where there should have been straight, smooth shin and even a man who was screaming unintelligible rants. It was fun watching the nurses maneuver him onto a bed on wheels and strap him in for everyone's protection.

"Follow me."

The hefty nurse in her faded purple scrubs took me down a fluorescent-lit hallway and to a little room where I sat on an electronic chair covered in paper that could have easily been used in a butcher shop in another situation.

"Wait here, someone will be in shortly."
"Thank you," I said, as the door was yanked shut.

Was my arm beginning to feel better, or was the pain fading as it became familiar? This thought played in my head as I waited for someone to come in and save me from the depressing sensation the room conjured.

"I'm Dr. Wells. What seems to be the problem Mister...Ryan?" Dr. Wells asked as she opened the door and scanned my paperwork.

"A guy on a bike ran me over."

"When did this take place?"

"This morning."

"And you didn't seek immediate medical attention?"

"I thought I was just being a baby. Now I'm wondering if something snapped in my wrist."

"Hold out your hand."

Extending my hand, the doctor's slender fingers gently rubbed my wrist and palm.

"Does that hurt?"

"It's uncomfortable. I wouldn't say it hurts exactly, but it doesn't feel normal."

"Does this hurt?" She asked, pushing against my palm and bending the hand back.

"*Yes, yes, yes!*"

"It's not broken. You may have a sprain or a hairline fracture. We'll do an X-ray to be sure. Please follow me."

Down more hallways of twists and turns, no wonder people in hospitals die, the faded white paint, peeling linoleum floor tiles and general lack of enthusiasm could kill anyone's spirit. Inside a room with a massive piece of machinery, a lead plated vest was provided to protect my body. Which didn't make sense, how much are you protecting me when you shoot X-rays through my arm?

The machine began buzzing and rotating around my outstretched arm, the doctor safely outside the room controlling the beast with a joystick of some sort. The ordeal ended quickly and I was left in another sad waiting room with several rambling patients in beds. If this was where they discharged people it must have been common for the discharge to involve a black bag and the morgue.

"The good news is that you don't have a fracture. Likely just a sprain. I'd recommend you grab an ace bandage from the drugstore and wrap your arm for a few days, keep ice on it tonight and wait for the swelling to go down," Dr. Wells advised.

This highly impressive treatment was going to cost a fortune once the insurance bill came. I knew I should have toughed it out and avoided the hospital. All along the remedy was at Duane Reade.

Thanking the doctor I provided a signature, collecting my belongings and heading for the exit. If this is what a day after a night in Queens is like, I would have to learn to control my drinking and start waking up on my own couch.

16. Splits

Things between Lacee and I remained tense after she stormed out of my apartment and back to the Bronx two weeks earlier. We exchanged a few texts back and forth but nothing serious. Until she asked if I wanted to grab lunch. Assuming the goal was to move past the issue I agreed, even though she asked if we could meet at her apartment. Lacee had a great apartment, but I was concerned her boyfriend or kids would be there.

Making it to the faraway land known as the Bronx, I walked from the train to 146th Street. The air was cool, a mist of rain wetting the skin of pedestrians as they scurried about in shorts and baggy shirts. Even though we were in the same city it was two drastically different worlds. The Upper East Side was little old ladies living off their dead husband's hard earned money. They moved from hair salon to butcher shop with dinged up silver walkers paying no mind to anyone.

The Bronx was loud. People on the street didn't wear headphones, forcing everyone to hear their hip-hop or rap music, I wasn't sure exactly which it was. They didn't seem to be going anywhere in the manner the old ladies of my neighborhood always were, people just appear to hang around here. It was a lot like where Lacee and I had lived in Brooklyn. It wasn't a bad area, but I could see someone robbing me in the dark. Crime was on the rise here after all, Brad had been running an errand for Lacee when three guys came up from behind, punched him in the head and stole his iPhone. He then made the mistake of chasing them and taking a much more brutal beating.

Lacee buzzed me in, I'd not been here since helping her move in and things looked the same. The same narrow staircase with the same blue carpet.

"Sorry I'm late, I didn't realize how far the train was," I said, Lacee letting me into the apartment.

I hid a scowl, the kids playing in the small room between the bedroom and living room. I heard them before looking to see them.

"Where's Brad?"

"He's working. Come in, do you want a towel, you're all wet?"

"No, I'll be dry in a minute. Is the babysitter here?"

"What babysitter?" Lacee's dark eyebrows raised at the question.

"Aren't we going to lunch?"

"I meant we could eat here. I have the kids and it's too hard to take them both out when Brad isn't around. Is that a problem?"

"No," I lied, hoping my face wouldn't give away the dissatisfaction being felt.

Had I known this was a play date I would have politely declined and suggested another time. Now I knew why Lacee wanted to meet at her apartment for the first time ever. It forced me to wonder if she was trying to punish me for our recent tiff.

"Did you want to order something?" I asked, wanting nothing more than to make lunch happen and get out of the apartment.

"Here, I have a few menus from places that are pretty good." Lacee handed over a dozen menus.

Each menu generic, other than the restaurant names, most of which were Chinese places, Happy-Something-Fun-Time or other. Picking the first one off the pile, I requested a beef and broccoli with white rice, Lacee placing the call. Through the speaker I could hear the giggling girl on the other end. Either Lacee ordered from this restaurant so often we were being mocked or the delivery girl had an uncontrollable need to laugh.

"Food should be here in about thirty minutes. Do you want some coffee?"

"Is that even a question?" I smiled, sitting at the square dining room table positioned against the wall across from the door. "Is this new?"

Lacee looked back from the counter where she was filling two white mugs with steaming coffee.

"Yeah, I got it as a birthday present for myself in May."
"Where's it from?" I asked, examining the dark finish of the wood.
"West Elm. I love that store."
"That must have set you back."
"It was only like nine hundred."

Nine-hundred dollars for a table? That was not only exorbitant it was insane when there was no way to host any type of party that didn't involve a dozen screaming children to put the table to good use.

"What's new with you?" Lacee asked, there was tension between us but she was clearly trying to move on.
"Things are pretty good. How about you?"
"Same drama, different day."
"Did you ever find out if anything is going on with Brad and that girl?"

Lacee's daughter, whose name was escaping my mind, ran into the room. Lacee placed her coffee cup on the table as the wild-haired child threw her body across Lacee's lap. She was asking for something but I couldn't make out the whispers.

"I'll be right back."

"Take your time." I sipped at my coffee hoping Lacee was going to pull a Mommy Dearest and strap the kid to a bed. I'd be happy to help with getting the wire hangers.

"Sorry, the movie ended. They should be occupied for another hour."

"Fun...so, the girl?"

"Oh, I decided to just let it go and stop prying."

"Why?"

"It's not doing any good and makes Brad and me fight more."

This was a rational approach. But to me it didn't make sense. If you are so convinced your boyfriend is cheating, and he has cheated in the past, how do you move on from that? Does it make Lacee a bigger person to accept the indiscretion and move on in life? Or does it make them both codependent and not dealing with the situation allowed life to go on while rage secretly built under the surface?

"That's impressive."

"It's called being in a relationship."

"I don't agree with that."

"Of course not, you're always single or dating a handful of people."

"Yes, but no one is making me live in a world of secrets."

"Let's not talk about it, you don't understand."

When people say to drop a subject, you don't understand or they don't want to talk about something, it's the equivalent of telling me to push until I get an answer. It's a reflex that I can't control. I'd like to blame it on being nosey, but it was probably more about my need to pull material out of people I could later splash across blank pages.

"Please, enlighten me."

Lacee was considering her response, biting at her bottom lip. Her flushed cheeks made the irritation clear.

"You want to know why you don't understand?"

"Absolutely."

"Fine, you don't understand because all you know how to do is pick at people until they go away. That's why your ex left you-"

"I left him," I interjected, needing to correct this inaccurate statement.

"Whatever, he cheated and was going to end up leaving you."

"Doesn't that logic apply to you and Brad?"

"No. Brad confessed and we're moving on."

"Once a cheater, always a cheater."

"He's not going to cheat again. But at least I have a relationship. You're going to be alone forever."

"What's wrong with being single?"

"Not single. Alone. You will drive everyone away and end up some sad, old gay man living by yourself in a tiny apartment."

The door buzzer rang cutting Lacee off and announcing the arrival of our food.

"I'm done with this."

"You're just going to leave?"

"You've done it. Now it's my turn."

"Are you going to pay for your food?"

"Here's a twenty," I said, tossing a wadded bill onto the overpriced table. "Chow down."

Pulling open the door, I hesitated. Perhaps the problem wasn't that Lacee and I had different views, but the reality of our lives moving in different directions. She was a mom with kids and maybe there was an obligation to make the relationship with Brad work. While I was single and my focus was to be successful and enjoy life.

"Maybe we should take a friend break," I said, not turning around.

"Fine by me."

Shutting the door I pushed past the delivery guy coming up the stairs. Lacee and I were at an impasse; maybe it was time for this relationship to end like so many others.

Arriving home I was more frustrated than when I left Lacee's apartment. Everything and everyone annoyed me on the way back. The crowded train car, the guy blasting music from his phone, people shoving through turnstiles, countless people bumping me at the subway exit. Like everyone in Manhattan knew I was pissed, they waited for this moment to make sure the day was miserable.

Tossing keys on the couch, the phone was buzzing in my back pocket. Pulling it out as I kicked off my shoes, the sudden cloud retraction outside bringing sun, heat and humidity. Every part of me was sweating. *New Message from Shew: Want to grab a drink?*

A drink was exactly what I needed right now. Since half of my friends were on hiatus from my toxic personality and me, it was probably a good idea to not refuse an invitation. Replying with acceptance and confirming a location in Hell's Kitchen for later that night I sent the message.

Crack. *Fuck! Oh, fuck!* Looking at my phone and not paying attention to where I was walking I jammed my foot into the leg of the couch. Pulling off the black sock, the two smaller toes were already swelling. Giving the baby toe a gentle squeeze, *fuck*; throbbing pains. Just as my wrist was recovering from the bike incident, I go and break two of my damn toes.

This was officially one of those days that needed to die. And what better way to lick my physical and emotional wounds than to drown them in alcohol.

17. Grabby

Hardware Bar was becoming a favorite spot. There was always a happy hour and when you arrived before nine there was hardly a soul in the place. If it weren't for the throbbing of my toes, internally screaming with each step, it would be the perfect evening.

Shew, who lived around the corner from the bar, was already seated on a stool behind the beer taps. The bar tried to live up to its name, the bar top itself a tarnished metal finish, the stools and tables square, bolts on the exterior to look raw. The walls covered in mirrors but a tint making it difficult to truly see the reflection of others. Wood slats lined part of the walls and the arched ceiling to appear as if we were in some secret tunnel where any filthy thing could happen.

"How are you?" I asked, sitting on the open stool beside Shew.

"Hey." We hugged briefly, me leaning forward to get the bartender's attention.

"What are you drinking?" I asked.

"Vodka soda," Shew replied, finishing a text before dimming his phone.

Vodka soda, one of the most popular drinks with the gay crowd. It must have been because of the low calories, I know it wasn't because of the taste.

"What can I get you?" asked the twink bartender, his tank top exposing a tribal tattoo that covered one shoulder and drifted onto his chest.

"What drinks are on happy hour?"

"Any of the bottled beers, bloody marys, mimosas and margaritas."

"Can I get a margarita?" There was no way I was passing up a happy hour margarita.

"Sure, on the rocks?"

"Can I do frozen?"

"No problem."

Once my drink arrived happy hour and the night could officially begin. Shew and I did the typical small talk, catching up on work and friends. I shared the recent mishaps with Business and the Animator, even delving into the day's drama with Lacee.

"I know I'll probably end up old and alone, but that doesn't mean I'm not right."

"Maybe she likes the drama," Shew suggested, polishing off vodka number three.

"Maybe. It's just so fucking stupid. You don't stay with a guy when he's banging other people." Maybe that fourth margarita was a bad idea. "Can I get a Bud Light?" I asked the bartender as he passed.

"Could she be cheating too?"

It was possible the reason Lacee was so unmoved by her boyfriend's cheating was because they had an open relationship. That could explain why she had been so quick to get off the subject and not want commentary.

"I doubt it. She's joked about cheating before, but I don't see her actually doing it."

"I wouldn't worry about it. You'll make up eventually."

Shew was probably right, Lacee and I had never really had a knockout fight before so it seemed overdue after being friends for a few years.

"Holy crap."

"What?" Shew asked, trying to get the bartender to come back and give him a lemon, his having landed on the floor.

"The Animator just text. He wants to hang out."

"Aren't you two not speaking?"

"Sounds like he's done being mad at me. Want to go to Duplex?"

"Sure, I guess."

Shew and I piled into a taxi, heading towards the Village to meet the Animator at my favorite dive piano bar. Duplex was the one bar I could count on to hear Stevie Nicks and other great music that had no place in today's trendy hot spots but would always be on my list of favorites.

Inside Duplex there was a significant crowd on the main level, the bar area crowded, the pianist cranking out some upbeat tune I'd never heard. Climbing the black, aging stairs to the upper level, only a few patrons scattered around the triangular space. The way I like a bar. A yellow glow lit the room, flaring from the giant letters hanging in the exposed windows to let the street below know what bar this was. The Animator sat alone, sipping what looked like a scotch. He was pale, more so than I'd ever seen him. His face a bit sunken as if he'd not eaten in a few days.

"Are you okay?" I asked, surprised to see my generally energetic friend look sullen.

"Yeah, what do you want to drink?"

"Just a beer."

The Animator ordered two beers, Shew and I sitting on either side of him. The leather cushion creaked as I wiggled to find a comfortable position.

"Look, I'm sorry if I offended you when-"

"You didn't offend me. It's fine."

"Okay, it's just that Business told me you're uncut and I thought maybe me bringing it up was an issue."

"How does Business know that? Actually, it doesn't matter. It's really fine, that night it wasn't about you."

"What was it about?" Probably none of my business, but I was drunk enough to not care.

"Gary and I...were about to have a threesome."

With vacant eyes I waited for the Animator to continue.

"I was nervous and when I answered the door it wasn't you I was expecting."

"Ooooh." Now things made sense, I'd killed the mood. "Did the threesome happen?"

"Not exactly. Gary passed out before the guy showed up."

"That's awkward."

"I sent the guy home, it would have been weird fucking him with Gary asleep next to us."

"That's noble."

"Why didn't you just go back to the other guy's place?" Shew asked, slumping on the bar, clearly approaching the point of way too much to drink.

"He lives in Brooklyn. I wasn't cabbing there and back."

"I retract my noble, and I like that you considered going to the guy's place until you knew he lived in Brooklyn," I said, gulping my beer.

"I should have just fucked him when I had the chance, not like it would have mattered."

"Why's that?" I asked.

"Gary and I broke up."

Not the answer I was expecting, shocking nonetheless.

"What happened? I thought things were going great." Being sympathetic was the hardest thing. I cared, but I wasn't good at being caring.

"They were. Gary has a little bit of a problem with meth and I couldn't handle it."

"That's a pretty big, *little problem*. I have an aunt and uncle that went to prison for a meth lab in their barn." My family is oddly colorful.

"I made him move out. If he can get his shit together I'd give it another try, but not until he pulls his head from his ass."

The admission explained why the Animator looked frail. As most people do when dating an addict they try to make things better by engaging in the activity with them, it never works. I learned this when I was young by watching my parents try to appease their respective spouses. People with addictions have to deal with it on their own, until they do there is no way out.

"I'm sorry." What else could be said? "Is there anything you need?"

"Just another drink," said the Animator, tossing back the remaining amber liquid in his stout glass.

Spending an hour with my friends drinking and joking made it possible to forget the recent drama. What was I so concerned about? Good friends always come back no matter what happens.

"It's probably time to call it a night," I said, pointing to Shew who was nearly asleep, face down on the bar.

"Yeah, I have to work tomorrow, probably a good idea."

Hailing a cab, I put a stumbling Shew in the backseat.

"Can you take him to fifty-fifth and eighth?"

"No, no, no. Get him out," roared the driver, straining his neck to see Shew in the back seat laying down.

"He's fine and he has cash." That was the magic word, cash.

The cab pulled forward to the light, waiting for the red to change and whisk Shew home. I said goodbye to the Animator, who lived within walking distance, hailing my own cab. Climbing in I looked back just in time to see Shew stumbling back onto the sidewalk. Shaking my head I told the driver where I was going.

The best part about going home alone was GrubHub. My favorite food app, promising to have food at my door within the hour. Delicious eggs, bacon and toast from the diner around the block. There was only a small amount of shame as the delivery guy arrived each time, his smile letting me know that I was secretly a fat kid. Placing my order, the cab pulled up to my building. Now all that was left was the wait.

In no time, my buzzer rang; I catapulted off the couch to press the button, unlocking the building's door. A tap at the door a few moments later, but to my surprise it wasn't my delivery guy with delicious shame food, it was Shew.

"What are you doing here?"

"You left me."

"What?"

"You left me on the street. I could have been robbed."

"You're clearly drunk." How did I end up the sober one? "I didn't leave you, you got out of the cab."

"Can I come in?" Shew asked, propping himself against the yellow doorframe. If I were into Jews, he would have been cute...and if he was sober that would help.

"Why?"

"Is someone here?"

"No," I replied, fully opening the door to reveal that it was only myself and the television in the apartment.

"Can I sit for a minute?"

"Fine, come in. I'm waiting for food anyway."

This was not how my post-bar-snack-time was supposed to play out. Not only was I now babysitting a twenty-five year old, he was going to want some of my food. Sharing was the last thing I wanted to do.

The buzzer rang again; this time I wanted to be sure it was the delivery guy.

"Who's there?" I asked into the intercom, holding the button for a response.

The words were impossible to understand, sounding like a microphone rubbing over concrete. It was close enough, I buzzed the person in. This time I waited with the door open; ready to rip the brown bag of delicious from the Spanish delivery guy's hands. Signing the credit card slip I thanked him and shut the door.

To my surprise Shew had drifted off while I stood at the door, ensuring there wouldn't be a war for food. I devoured the meal. Exactly how every night would end if I wasn't worried about becoming fat and nobody wanting to stick it in ever again.

Brushing my teeth, I turned off the light, putting a blanket on Shew before climbing into bed.

When someone gropes you on the train you pretend it didn't happen and try to move on. It's much more surprising when you wake up and one of your friends has a hand wrapped around your dick. Literally yanking me from sleep, Shew was beside me in bed, slowly stroking me.

Unsure of what to do at first, grabbing his hand, pushing it away. A few minutes passing and the hand returned, rubbing my side with just one cold finger.

"Stop," I hissed, was this really happening?

A few more hand slaps and I figured Shew had gotten the message. He rolled over, providing me peace. That was until rolling back over, straddling me and beginning a dry hump. Pushing at his thighs I realized his pants weren't on. This was bad; I was only in my underwear, not providing much of a barrier between our flesh.

One hand on my chest and the other maneuvering me out of my underwear, Shew made to sit on my dick. Was this rape? With one of my hands pinned under his knee and the other trying to push him off while pulling up my underwear we made contact. For a brief moment there was penetration.

Taking a drastic measure I thrust forward, turning my body to knock him off the bed and me. Shew hit the floor with a hard thump.

"Go home."

"What?" Shew asked, as if he'd done nothing.

"Get out of here or I swear to god, I'm going to deck you in the face."

"Don't get mad."

"GET OUT!"

Shew put his clothes on, holding open the door I was ensuring his prompt exit.

"You left me on the street."

"Shut up and go home," I said, how are we back on this topic.

"You're an asshole. I hope you enjoy getting fucked by some guy from Tool Box."

Rent (minus) Control: Turning Thirty

The random insult referenced the old man gay bar a half-dozen blocks up the street. With no idea where he was getting the gull to toss insults I shut, locked and chained the door. I could hear Shew's rants until the elevator doors closed. That's the moment my phone began blowing up with text messages from him.

While turning my phone to silent I noticed a missed text from Business. *6 more days.* Talk about bad timing.

18. Cut

With my birthday now in the very near future it was time to clean up my messes. With two of three friendships back to normal I needed to deal with my dating life. West and Leo were both still on the table, one interested in a relationship and getting no sex, the other interested in only sex and getting what he desired.

I was determined to exit my twenties with less chaos than I entered and lived them. The last decade was one to be remembered. A list of learned life lesson longer than I could recount, enough drama to create an epic mini-series and many, many men.

Lacee's words had stuck with me, forcing me to think about if I wanted to be alone or if a relationship was the better path. Ready to put forward the issue with West, I asked him out to breakfast. We met in a new diner near his apartment. How he lives on 42nd Street I will never understand. So close to Times Square, the center of tourist hell.

"I'm glad to see you, it's been a while," West said, climbing into the booth across from me.

"You too. I know I vanished for a bit. I just needed some time to think."

"You ready to order?" a waiter appeared from somewhere, notepad in hand, toothpick in mouth. We were apparently in the 1950's.

"Can I start with a coffee?" I said, picking up the menu.

"Same."

"Anything to eat?"

"Can we have a few minutes?" West asked.

The waiter rushed away, vanishing through swinging doors, hopefully not to spit in our coffee for being unprepared.

"So things are good?" West asked, putting his hand on mine from across the table.

I nodded. Why is it so hard to tell someone what you're feeling? Oh, that's right, I loathe feelings.

"I wasn't sure I was going to hear from you again?"

"Why?"

"The last time you came over, you left so fast."

"Yeah, that."

The last time I saw West was after seeing a Joan Rivers show with Dimitri and Larry. After the show we stopped at 9th Avenue Saloon where there was a dollar drink special. Loading up on Sraw-brrr-itas I was properly intoxicated by the time the two of them grabbed a cab back to Queens. Not ready to go home, feeling frisky and on Eighth Avenue it seemed logical to drop in on West.

We made out on his sofa, me grinding all over him and giving the definite impression that he was going to get lucky. But the moment he turned me onto my back, gazing down, I thought I was going to be sick. Not because of him, but because the number of drinks sloshing around my stomach. My head was beginning to spin, stomach lurching as if I might vomit.

Instead of staying to embarrass myself or have terribly clumsy sex, I made up an excuse to leave. Rushing out of the apartment I hailed cab, stuck my head between my knees and prayed to make it home without puking all over the torn leather seat.

"I was really drunk."

"I know, I liked it." West smiled.

"It wasn't you, I thought that I might get sick from the drinks and didn't want you to see if I did."

"It's fine, but I wish you had stayed."

It was time to admit that there was no way I could stay. I'd spent one night at his apartment, deflecting his many suggestive moves. A herculean task when you're acting like a horny teenager.

"I have to say something to you and I hope you don't get terribly offended."

West sat his coffee on the table, his eyes the color of honey in the light. He looked to be holding his breath, a visible worry that I was going to reveal an unpleasant personal truth.

"I'm afraid to see your penis."

"Excuse me?"

"When we first met you mentioned you have foreskin."

"Yeah."

"I've really only ever seen an uncut one twice in my life and it freaks me out. I was worried if I saw your penis I might not like it, or it would be awkward and I didn't know how to deal with it other than not having sex with you."

"Wait, you haven't had sex with me because I'm uncut?" West's concerned face was now twisted.

"Yes," I murmured, wanting to crawl under the table where he couldn't see me.

"I thought you were taking your time, moving slow. I thought it was sweet."

"I did want to move slow."

"Wow, I feel like an idiot." West began digging in his pocket.

"It's not you."

"No, it's you."

That shut me up. Apparently we agreed on one thing.

"I've met a lot of shallow guys since I moved to New York, but you're something else." West put a few singles on the table.

"Don't leave," I pleaded as he got up from the table.

"I'm really disappointed by your immaturity. I thought you were different." West put his hand on the table, leaning in, he was either going to kiss me or head-butt me. "You string me along like this may turn into something, when all the while you were just playing a game. I hope you find what you're looking for, it's not me."

There was nothing I could say. West was right, I had played a game with him, intentional or not. It was only fair that he have the last word, not that I had any words left to say. He left, tossing a fist of crumpled dollars on the table.

"I know your birthday isn't for three more days but I thought it would be nice if we celebrated today since I won't be able to see you Wednesday," said Business, at my door with a box of Baked by Melissa cupcakes.

"Right now I love and hate you," I announced, extracting one of the mini cupcakes from the box he was holding open. "You realize I'll have to throw this up later."

"That or just drink enough to forget you ever ate it."

"You're an evil genius."

Business not only brought cupcakes but a bottle of Malbec, this was shaping up to be a pleasant pre-birthday surprise. Pouring two glasses I joined Business on the couch where he was halfway through the decadent pastries.

"Happy early birthday," Business raised his glass.

"Thank you."

"I have to admit this isn't a totally selfless visit."

"Are you going to make me pay for the cupcakes?" I asked, ready to spit the half-eaten chocolate out of my mouth.

"No, of course not. I have some news that I wanted to tell you."

"You're pregnant?"

"I'm thankful every day that I don't have a vag for that reason alone."

"Amen," I said, clinking our glasses together. "What's the big news?"

Business put forward a hand.

"You got a manicure?"

"No," he beamed, wiggling a finger with a silver ring.

"I'm not following." Was the ring new?

"Drew asked me to marry him."

"Oh my god." I was blindsided by the revelation. "Congratulations." Did that sound sincere?

"Thanks. I know you're not big on marriage, but I had to tell someone."

"When did all of this happen?"

"He asked last night at dinner. There's this great Italian place between our apartments, he rented the whole thing. I thought it was dead when we arrived, but when our meals came he got down on one knee and asked."

"I'm happy for you," I said, giving Business a hug.

None of my friends had ever been engaged, at least none of my New York friends, this was something I hadn't dealt with since I moved away from Utah. I wasn't clear on what to say or the questions to ask. If Business was a girl I could ask about the dress and location, that's what you hear in movies, but what do you ask when people get gay engaged?

"Do you know when you're getting married?" I probed, hoping it was what he wanted to hear, and not too soon.

"Probably before the holidays."

"That's fast."

"It's not going to be anything big. We're just going to hit City Hall and be done with it. It's not like one of us can be marching down an aisle in a white dress."

"You can, it just makes it a different type of affair." I couldn't miss an opportunity to poke fun.

"I'm telling you because I wanted to ask if you would be our witness."

"What's that?"

"You just come to City Hall and sign the paper."

"That doesn't make me married, right?"

"You know, it's just so we have someone close to us, someone closer than the random judge."

"You know I will, I'm happy to."

"Great. Well, I actually have to get back home, we're going to tell Drew's parents."

"Have you told your parents?"

"Are you kidding, they still don't know I'm gay, we aren't telling them."

"How does Drew feel about that?" I asked, wondering how it worked if one groom was closeted to his family and the other wasn't.

"We're still working out the details, but it'll be fine," Business explained, attempting to convince us both. "Enjoy the wine and the rest of these, I have to go or I'll be late."

"I hate you for leaving me with these."

"You'll burn it off at the gym tomorrow."

Business gave me a hug before rushing off down the hallway. I watched, wondering why it was so easy for some people to open up to others while the rest of us avoid connecting.

19. Happy

Celebrating a birthday has never been something I shied away from, even after all the stress instilled by the constant reminders of moving from a twenty-something to a thirty-something my friends helped me make the best of things.

After Business' marital confession kicked things off with calorie-loaded cupcakes, I found myself bar hopping with the Animator. Regaling him with the tale of Shew and the hand job of doom, leaving out certain parts to hide my own embarrassment. We drank at a number of bars on the Lower East Side, testing the true capacity of our livers. This resulted in a night with my face in the toilet, passing out and eventually waking up as my arm throbbed with pain.

Drunk to the point of disorientation I made a bed face down on the bathroom floor. This is why people buy fuzzy bathroom rugs, it's as close to a security blanket as you can get after age eight. Properly wearing the Animator out with my binging, I made my way to the next circle of friends.

Rent (minus) Control: Turning Thirty

Dimitri and Larry didn't work evenings like the Animator, making it that much easier to meet them around nine and have all night benders that ended only with bars flipping on lights and forcing us into the street. It's amazing how quickly time passes when you're having a good time. This wouldn't be a bad thing, except doing it two nights in a row, on weekdays, has to be the most painful way.

If it hadn't been my birthday, and I wasn't a general bad influence, my friends would have made responsible decisions and gone home to bed so they could get up for work in the morning. Instead, we went all out, drinks and coke from Hell's Kitchen's favorite dealer, Baby, and many more drinks. With this little bag of energy it was possible to dance the night away without the alcohol telling your brain, *'you've had more than enough.'*

Somewhere in the midst of all this erratic fun I had a text exchange with Leo. I didn't recall until scanning through the messages on my phone the morning of my actual birthday. He asked what I was up to the night before, obviously out killing my liver, I told him we were all celebrating my birthday. I failed to invite him, which would have been a good idea as it's almost a definite that we would have gone home together; damn. His final message stated he was taking me to dinner and to not make plans on my official birthday.

In a perfect world I would exchange the dinner plans for drinks and sex, but I was excited by the offer. Actually, this could even be classified as giddy. Maybe the little crush I thought I had was being reciprocated.

Once my hangover passed, I reached out to Leo to see where he wanted to meet. Rather than having a plan he asked if there was anywhere I wanted to try. Searching a few places on the web he refuted them all. After my third option was rejected I suggested we meet at Patron's in HK around nine. He said that worked since he was having happy hour drinks at seven with two friends around the corner from there.

Overeager, I arrived at Patron half an hour early, but this was no problem.

"Can I get a frozen strawberry margarita? The big one."

"This one?" asked the bartender, holding up a chalice the size of my head.

"Yes, please." I could feel the grin across my face; this place had the best, strongest, margaritas.

Downing the frozen deliciousness, I checked my phone. *New Message from Leo: Where are you?* I was right where I said I would be. *Why are you there?* Because we agreed this is where we were going to meet. *I never agreed to meet there. Do you want to come here? We just ordered food.* Are you kidding me? I gave a time and address to which there was no objection, how is that not agreeing to meet somewhere?

I waited until Leo was done with his friends, finishing another large, fruit flavored margarita as well as starting on a smaller, more respectably sized one. This was the moment that Leo chose to arrive. He grabbed my waist, probably intending to be cute, but jolting me, as I wasn't expecting a strange hand to grab at me.

"You made it," I said, sucking on my strawberry filled straw.

"You should have come to Therapy."

"I wasn't up for meeting your friends and pretending to be interesting."

"You're drunk."

"Yes, I am." Were my words coming out slurred? It was hard to tell.

"What do you want to do?"

"I'm going to finish this drink. Would you like one?"

"Do you really need that drink?"

"I really do."

Finishing my drink and settling the tab, eighteen-dollars apiece, good thing those giant margaritas are strong, we made our way to the sidewalk. The night was warm, meaning street traffic was high. A fence along the edge of the road for construction was causing sidewalk traffic to condense along with the tables restaurants placed outside to attract people. It was an all-out shove-fest.

"Are you hungry?" Leo asked.

"Didn't you just eat?" Why was he eating with his friends at a bar when he invited me out to dinner?

"I ate a little, I could eat something small."

"You didn't like any of my restaurant selections, is there somewhere you want to go?"

"There's VYNL over there or there's Eatery."

"I don't care, pick one."

"Let go to Eatery, I was at VYNL last week."

Following Leo to the corner, Eatery was packed. The romantic ambiance created by candlelit tables and a purple glow radiating from an unidentified source were overpowered by the close proximity of the tables to our left and right. We were so close to our neighbors that I was being drawn into their conversations. The girl on my left boring her date with tales of her apartment and how she 'feng shuied' the place. The girl on my right crying into her napkin. Is this what straight couples do on dates? No wonder they get pregnant and divorced so often.

"Can I take your drink order?" asked our handsome waiter.

"Can I get a vodka martini?"

"I'll just have water," I said, knowing that I needed to slow down or I was going to be a drunken fool.

"Now you don't want a drink?" Leo prodded.

"Not for the moment."

The waiter was speedy, my water appearing along with the martini, me doing some magic of my own and draining the glass. The bus boy appeared as I returned the glass to its stationary position. Filling it to the brim, it was clear this was a competition. He was going to top off my glass every time I sipped, meaning I would have a compulsive need to keep drinking to try and drain the glass before he made his way back.

"Anything to eat, gentlemen?"

"Can I get the Chicken Alfredo?"

"Of course, and for you sir?"

"Nothing for me."

I waited for the waiter to walk away before opening my mouth.

"If you're not eating then why are we here?"

"You're hungry."

"No, I said I could eat because I thought that was the plan. If you're not going to eat I'd rather just go have a drink somewhere."

"I can't get trashed."

"I'm not saying to get trashed, I'm saying let's go have a drink."

"You're not being very respectful."

What the fuck is he talking about? How am I not being respectful by saying I'd rather go have a good time instead of spending fifty-dollars on a meal I don't want?

"Respectful of what?"

"I have to get up early in the morning for an interview."

"What time is your interview?" I asked.

"Eleven."

"It's not even ten yet. You're telling me you can't have a drink because you'll be too drunk to get up for something that's thirteen hours away?"

"You don't understand. All you do is sit home checking emails all day."

All I wanted to do was punch him in the face. To avoid acting on the impulse I sat on my hands. Leo struck a chord with his statement; he didn't know anything about my work life or me. Not that I knew much about his, but I wasn't the one calling him out. My second impulse was to get up and walk out, but that was something I did in my twenties and I wasn't going to carry that over to my thirties.

My food eventually arrived, declining a proper drink once more. Eating in silence, I did so as quickly as possible. It was time to get out of here and end this god-awful date.

"Can we get the check?" Leo asked as the waiter passed by and I put down my utensils.

Usually I would offer to split the check, but in this instance he could pay. He invited me out, and in my mind screwed up the night, the check was all his.

Again outside, I didn't know what to say.

"What do you want to do now?" Leo asked.

"I think I'm ready to call it a night," I answered, avoiding his gaze.

"Don't leave yet."

"What's the point in hanging around?"

"I don't want you to leave mad at me."

"It's a little late for that."

"Look, I'm sorry I pissed you off. Let's just start over and go have a drink at Industry."

They say that men think with their dicks, that statement is tragically true. Agreeing to one more drink we walked around the corner. Ordering us each a beer I paid the bartender, finding Leo waiting against the wall on a raised bench.

"Here," I said, thrusting a bottle forward.

"Thanks."

Trying to detach from the situation I began to dance in place to the throbbing music. It was still my birthday and I wasn't going to let a bad date, or the boring crowds ruin it for me. I danced, sipping at my beer, letting go of the irritation, slowly starting to feel better. This did nothing to sway the crowd, everyone standing around like fixtures unable to move for fear of not looking cool.

Polishing off my beverage I turned to ask a still sitting Leo if he wanted another. But that question had no merit, his beer was completely full.

"Are you ready to go?" I asked, putting the empty brown bottle on the nearest table, all of the irritation of the restaurant rushing back.

"Sure, if you are."

Bolting through the frosted glass of the double doors we were right back where we started.

"Do you want to come over?" Leo asked.

Considering the night was an epic failure, the least we could do was salvage it with good sex. Following him into a cab we made our way to his apartment. The cab ride is always longer when you're drunk, each block passing slower than the last.

By the time we arrived at Leo's apartment he was nodding off. Jabbing him in the side he woke, swiping a card to pay the fare. Leading me through the faded red doorway and up the brown stairs. Numbers once declaring the floor of the building was missing, a two imprinted in the paint, screw holes looking out like curious black eyes.

Winded by the top of the third flight of stairs, even the nipping dog didn't bother me when we entered the apartment. I needed to sit down and get my shoes off. Taking a moment to undress and hit the bathroom, I flicked off the living room light, tiptoeing down the long hallway. Leo's feet were all I could see as I approached, already on the bed.

A surprise waited for me when I finally reached the bedroom. Leo was out like a light, snoring, clearly this wasn't happening.

Rather than crawl in bed next to the man I was crushing on and continue to fume I decided it was better to leave. The night had gone wrong in ways I couldn't have imagined, clearly we were not a match, sex not enough to make anything worth the effort. The dog bit at my ankles as I redressed. Slipping out the door I closed it softly to not disturb the sleeping, making my way down the stairs and out of this place.

20. Credits

Certain birthdays are milestones in life that make you feel different. Sixteen gives you freedom from begging people to cart you around. Eighteen gives you freedom from being told what to do. Twenty-one gives you freedom from going to jail for the alcohol you've been consuming for years. Twenty-five gives you the freedom to live in New York and rent a car when you need to make a long trip to IKEA.

Thirty was providing me a new kind of freedom. I wasn't looking for love like so many of my friends. I realized I had all of the relationships in place I needed to sustain a happy life. With that I was letting go of nicknames, a defense mechanism I used since my first heartbreak to keep people at arm's length. And things were actually calm for a change.

No dramatic guys in my life forcing my head to spin while trying to understand why they do the things they do. No friends telling me who or how to be. And no regrets. Everything in my life was exactly how I wanted and needed.

"Hello, I'm here to see Mr. Wright."

"Your name please," said the receptionist. Her soft brown hair and pale blue eyes looking polite. I wonder if she's putting on an act or truly this sweet.

"Robert Ryan. I have an appointment at two."

"I'll let him know you're here," she said, picking up a phone, poking at the many blinking buttons.

Play House Books was a far cry from Silver Publishing, it wasn't a surprise that my former editor Emily wasn't able to survive here. On the sixteenth floor of a glass and steel tower downtown, it was clear that the authors of this publisher were successful.

"Mr. Ryan, Mr. Wright is ready for you. Down the hallway, second door on the right."

"Thank you," I answered, grabbing my bag, marching down the hallway.

The white walls were decorated in photos of book covers and articles on the authors to showcase their talent and the publisher's impressive portfolio.

"Fuck you, you fucking traitor."

Turning around a familiar, fake British accent was calling in my direction.

"Emily. What are you doing here?"

"They just fired me. No thanks to you."

"I though they fired you forever ago?" What was going on here?

"They fired me because the one author on my roster abandoned me for that sleazy cunt, Wright."

"No, he met me at our last meeting and said you had been let go."

"You fucking moron, you should have picked up a phone to confirm."

Emily's rant continued, her anger overflowing onto everyone that passed us in the hallway. That was until two security guards appeared, taking her under the arms.

"Don't touch me, fucking clods." This was the first time I heard Emily break her accent and speak in her real, American voice. "Fuck all of you. I'm going to burn this fucking building down. You're all fucking trash." There was the Jersey girl we all knew was in there.

Arriving at the closed door of the editor that had apparently stolen me out from under Emily, I rapped lightly on the door.

"Come in, come in. So good to see you," said John, propping open the door and directing me to a plastic red chair in front of his far-too-big office desk.

The space was much more impressive than anything Emily had ever known. What I guessed were mahogany bookshelves lined the wall behind John's desk; books of every size and color filled the shelves. A window to the right made up the entire wall overlooking the East River, the Brooklyn Bridge visible. John's desk was well organized, not cluttered with paper like Emily's desk always was. His laptop propped open on the corner, a notepad and pen in front of him and ready for action.

"What do you have for me today Robert?"

"It's Ryan."

"Yes, yes, sorry about that, I forgot. What do you have for me?"

"I've completed the manuscript," I said, pulling from my bag the printed manuscript, ready for review and what was likely to be heavy criticism. "It's a little different from what was requested."

"How so?" John folded his hands into one another, leaning back in the high-back black leather chair.

"When I started it was all about making things dirtier than the last installment. Emily said to add sex, sex, sex and that's what I was doing. Halfway through I knew the book didn't have any guts. It was a catalogue of sexual adventures. What I realized was that I'm not the sum of the people I sleep with. There's a lot more to the story."

"Good for you. I'm glad you broke from Emily's advice and wrote what you felt was best."

"You are?" I'd anticipated a reprimanding for breaking from the prescribed formula.

"Yes. Let me explain," said John, leaning forward, elbows on the desk, clasped hands under his square chin. "Emily was terrible for your career. I see so much potential in your writing, but as long as she was leading the way you were never going to achieve another best seller."

"I thought you said my last book wasn't doing well."

"I wasn't completely honest with you."

A feeling in the pit of my stomach said that I was about to have my book contract revoked and this manuscript was headed for the trash bin.

"*Rent minus control* isn't a best seller yet, but it's climbing the charts and we've even requested a second printing."

"What?" A second printing?

"Between us, I needed Emily out the door. Over the past six months I've been altering your book sales. Not exactly ethical, but it's a cutthroat world out there."

"This doesn't make any sense, I've been getting checks for almost nothing. If the book is doing well, where's the money?"

"Here." John pulled an envelope from a drawer, extending it over the desk.

Taking the white envelope, I opened the flap to glance inside. A check with more zeroes than I'd ever been handed now before me.

"That's the reaction I was hoping for. With Emily out of the picture, I guarantee your new book can be a New York Times best seller within the first six months. All you have to do is sign."

John placed a document and pen on the desk. A new publishing contract that would put him in charge of the marketing and distribution of my work. Glancing over the familiar language I added my signature in the bottom corner along with the date.

"Great. I'll take the manuscript if I may."

Handing John the pages that defined the last year of my life, this was almost surreal. Suddenly it felt that I was less of an unknown author and someone who had a shot at making it big.

"I look forward to reading..." John looked at the front of the manuscript. "*Turning Thirty*, and letting you know what I think. I should have notes back to you next week along with any necessary changes."

"That's fine."

Rising from my chair, a bit dazed, I paused with the door's knob in hand.

"John."

"Yes, sir?"

"I appreciate what you've done for me, even if it was ethically questionable."

"Any time." John beamed, proud of his backstabbing tactics.

"That said, after this book is released I won't be seeking another contract with this publishing house."

"Excuse me?"

"Between you and Emily it has helped me find my voice and discover a lot about myself. It's time to write something that isn't just about selling books."

"You're making a mistake." John stood, hoping to help me see the light.

"Possibly, but I'd rather make a mistake than garner more success at the expense of other people."

With a light smile, I left the office. I'd be back again when the book was released, but for now the future was mine and no one, not even a pushy editor, was going to tell me how to write it.

Other Works

The Other Realm
The Other Realm: Blood Vengeance
The Anomaly
Rent (minus) Control

For more information visit: www.rbwinters.com

Synopsis

Year-after-year people eagerly indulge in life milestones, but turning thirty is one event that shakes most twenty-somethings to their core. You're old enough to know better, but still young enough to land flat on your face. Ryan's cynical nature has carried him this far in life, but as his world begins to change it's going to take a lot of friends and wine to come out the other side.

www.ingramcontent.com/pod-product-compliance
Lightning Source LLC
Chambersburg PA
CBHW050939120626
46552CB00001B/282